Praise for Joseph Flynn and his novels

Digger

"A mystery cloaked as cleverly as (and perhaps better than) any John Grisham work."
— *Denver Post*

"Engrossing ... non-stop action and original plot ... rapid-fire suspense."
— Phillip Margolin
New York Times Bestselling Author of Wild Justice

"A deftly mapped thriller. Page-turner of the week."
— *People Magazine*

"A straightforward, pulse-pounding novel ... a forceful hard-boned book."
— Carsten Stroud
New York Times Bestselling Author of *Deadly Force*

"Mix Dashiell Hammet's *Red Harvest* and T*he X-Files* and you'll get some idea of how original this concept is. Recommended book."
— Thriller Editor, *amazon.com*

"An exciting, gritty, emotional page-turner."
— Robert K. Tanenbaum
New York Times Bestselling Author of *True Justice*

"Surefooted, suspenseful, and in its breathless final moments, unexpectedly heartbreaking."
— *Booklist*

The Next President

"Flynn [is] a master of high-octane plotting."
— *Chicago Tribune*

"Flynn keeps the pages turning in this well-done thriller."
— *Houston Chronicle*

"An original, suspenseful thriller that will keep you turning the pages."
— *amazon.com*

"A thriller that's fast enough to keep reading straight through (in) one sitting."
— *Rocky Mountain News* (Denver)

"(A) tough, stylish tale ... (Flynn) propels his plot with potent but flexible force, using just the right mix of pressure and release to maintain suspense deep into the story."
— *Publishers Weekly*

"Readers raved about this book ... cat and mouse suspense ... full of twists ... a well-written, timely thriller. Highest marks."
— *Barnes & Noble Guide to New Fiction*

"Flynn is an excellent storyteller with a well-tuned ear for dialogue and a gift for creating memorable characters placed in believable settings ... *The Next President* bears favorable comparison to such classics as *The Best Man, Advise and Consent*, and *The Manchurian Candidate*."
— *Booklist*

Gasoline, Texas

Laddy Johnson may or may not be the unacknowledged love child of the late President Lyndon Baines Johnson. But one thing's for sure: After fifteen years of being a Hollywood stuntman, Laddy's come back to run for mayor of his hometown of Gasoline, Texas.

His opponent is incumbent Edwin "Win-Win" Winslow. Win-Win is the quintessential Texas good ol' boy. A former star lineman at Texas A&M, Win-Win now owns Texas Rolling Stock, an upscale SUV dealership that sells internal combustion monsters like gas was still 25¢ a gallon.

Which in Gasoline it still is. The town has its own oil field and refinery. And the Municipal Field is what the election is all about. Laddy vows to keep it. Win-Win wants to sell it to Big Oil, which is getting nervous about the idea of anybody in the country still having access to affordable fuel. Win-Win promises that every homeowner in town will get a windfall payment that will make the sale a good deal. Laddy cautions that Big Oil is way too slippery to trust.

Who will win? Will the Winslow dynasty be extended another generation? Will Laddy ever find out who his daddy is? Will he marry his first love, now a famous movie star? Or will he chuck everything to take up with Win-Win's long lost daughter, Hayley?

Finding out is a gusher of fun.

By Joseph Flynn

The Concrete Inquisition
Digger
The Next President
Hot Type

Farewell Performance

Joseph Flynn

Stray Dog Press, Inc.
SPRINGFIELD, IL
2007

Published by Stray Dog Press, Inc.
Springfield, IL 62704, U.S.A.

First Stray Dog Press, Inc. Printing, June 2007

Visit the author's web site: www.josephflynn.com

Flynn, Joseph
    Farewell Performance / Joseph Flynn.
    221 p.
    ISBN 978-0-9764170-3-3

Printed in the United States of America

PUBLISHER'S NOTE
This is a work of fiction. Names, characters, places, and incidents either are the product of the author's imagination or are used fictitiously; any resemblance to actual persons, living or dead, events, or locales is entirely coincidental.

Book design by Aha! Designs
Typeface: Adobe Caslon

For Caitie
A gift beyond measure.

Acknowledgments

My thanks to Ryan Dougherty,
Meghan Dougherty, and C. R. Flynn
for giving an old Boomer
some sense of currency
regarding today's popular culture.

Farewell Performance

CHAPTER 1

Monday

They met at the Rose Café in Venice, two cops trying to look like civilians, not quite pulling it off. That was the impression they got anyway, the way other diners strolling out onto the restaurant's patio kept their distance. Had to be some subtle suggestion of covert authority and concealed weapons. Otherwise, two good-looking people like them, they'd be jostling for elbow room.

Joan Duarte's sable hair fell to her shoulders and framed an oval face that Modigliani would have loved to paint. She would turn 40 in two months, but her trim figure clad in jeans, a pink polo shirt and an unstructured pearl white linen jacket said she was ten years younger. Rick Valkonen was obviously older, mid-50s, but he was no less striking than his companion. Tall and lean with a craggy face, he had sapphire blue eyes and wavy hair that intertwined threads of gold and silver. His jeans were faded and topped by a new baggy black sweatshirt, bereft of designer logo, university affiliation, or lowbrow witticism.

Detective Duarte was with the Santa Monica Police Department; Sergeant Valkonen was LAPD. Even sitting at the café table after introducing themselves, they gave off the feeling of two dogs circling one another, unsure of which one would lunge first.

Maybe that was what kept people away.

Duarte took a sip of her Arrowhead sparkling water and said, "My boss said to tell you our department will be happy to cooperate with LAPD in any way it can."

Valkonen grinned. He rolled his coffee cup back and forth between his hands.

"Let me be honest with you, Detective. I got assigned to this job because I'm on *my* boss's shit-list. And you've been told who my boss is, right?"

"LAPD's new chief," she said. "Thomas Barton."

"Yeah. So pardon me if I'm wrong, but if I got stuck with this thing for screwing up, I have to wonder why you're here this morning."

Duarte looked at the cup of coffee Valkonen was still playing with. Black coffee, as simple as you could make it. But what she noticed most was his hands. They were big and strong, nails closely trimmed. Made her think that lean or not this guy had some good muscle under that loose shirt of his. Made her wonder, too, what kind of sidearm he carried under there.

She looked up at him and said, "You tell me your screw-up, I'll tell you mine."

"Fair enough," he said. He took a sip of his coffee and put the cup down, off to one side. "I proved to be a lousy babysitter."

Duarte looked at him like he was jerking her around, but he held his hands up to placate her.

"God's truth. My final assignment before I retire after 30 years of service was to babysit the chief's son, keep him out of trouble here in temptation city."

"Your chief has twins, right? Didn't I read that in the paper?"

"Boy and a girl, 16. Normally, I watch Justin and Sergeant Mary Pat Keegan watches Justine. But this past weekend, Justin comes down with the sniffles and he's in bed for the weekend. I think, great, time off for me. But Keegan wants to go to San Francisco for her favorite niece's wedding, begs me to watch Justine, swears she'll make it up to me." Valkonen shook his head. "Like a sucker, I say okay."

"Bad move, huh?"

"Well, with Justin, if need be, I can go into the men's room with him. With Justine, I have to trust she won't get in trouble making wee-wee all on her own."

"She did? What'd she do, ditch you?"

Valkonen nodded.

"Not out a window."

"No. The little princess was slicker than that. She had some kid waiting in the john for her. Slipped her a new jacket, a hat, a different pair of sunglasses. When she came out with her hair tucked up under the hat and the new shades, I didn't recognize her. My bad. I should have picked up on her fat backside, except I try not to notice those things on girls that young."

Duarte laughed and nodded.

"Good for you, Sergeant."

"Yeah. Anyway, she gets away clean. I finally show my badge to a lady who's about to use the facilities and ask if she'll see if there's a young girl named Justine in there. She comes out about ten seconds later with the clothes the kid was wearing and a note that was with them, says: *Ha-ha.* Real charmer, that kid."

"She didn't get hurt when she was out on her own, did she?" Duarte asked.

"I'll get to that in a minute. Now, you tell me what you did."

"I hit a cop."

"In anger?"

"In retaliation. He swung at me first."

"Why'd he do that?" Valkonen asked.

Duarte sighed.

"The guy had been sexually harassing me for months."

"You report him?"

They both knew this was a sensitive decision. A female cop who filed such a complaint always found it hard to get any male cop to work with her again. They were afraid she might falsely accuse them of the same thing.

Then again, there were cops who felt the only reason to have a female partner was if she was putting out for you.

So there was justifiable heat in Duarte's voice when she said, "Damn right, I did."

"And?"

"And I couldn't prove it. Bastard was always real sneaky about it. He'd come up behind me and whisper filthy things in my ear. Not loud enough for anyone else to hear."

"He ever touch you inappropriately?"

The detective's jaw tightened and she nodded.

"And nobody saw that?"

"Not that they'd be willing to say officially."

Valkonen shook his head.

"So what happened? You got this guy to lash out at you?" he asked.

"My lawyer gave me the idea. She said give him some of his own medicine, demean him when I thought the time was right. Opportunity came during a shift change; I was heading out, into the parking lot, he was heading into the station. He gave me this big smile because he'd just been cleared of the charges I'd filed against him. I noticed right then he and I were the only cops present who spoke Spanish. So I said a few things. Nasty, terrible things. But in this sugar-sweet voice like I'd just come from charm school."

Duarte smiled at the memory.

"That's when he tried to hit you," Valkonen said.

"He *ran* at me swinging. Bastard punches like a pansy. I punch like my dad, and he was a Golden Gloves champ. Blackened the creep's eye and knocked him on his ass with one shot. But that wasn't the worst thing."

"No, what was?"

"He wet himself. Sat there in his own stink. Nobody wanted to help him up. It became a he said/she said thing since nobody but us understood what I'd said. We both got conduct-unbecoming flags in our personnel files and we were suspended without pay for a week."

"You didn't fight that?"

"I'd already given my lawyer enough money. I thought about quitting but I've got 17 years in. I want my pension. I came back to work this morning and they told me go see this cop from LAPD. So here I am. What'd Justine do after she got away from you?"

"She ran into this kid in Santa Monica who told her about a free concert that's supposed to happen soon."

"That's it?"

"Well, the thing is, the band is supposed to kill themselves — onstage."

Duarte's jaw dropped.

"Yeah, and when the music stops, everybody in the audience is supposed to commit suicide, too. And they're expecting a crowd of maybe a thousand kids."

"That has to be bullshit ... doesn't it?"

"Well, Detective, that's what you and I have to find out."

CHAPTER 2

The café got crowded enough that people overcame their inhibitions and took tables close to Duarte and Valkonen. The two cops didn't want their conversation overheard so they moved on to Palisades Park in Santa Monica where they walked and talked. The homeless people hanging out in the park saw them coming and had no doubts they were cops; they moved along before Duarte and Valkonen got within ten yards of them.

The joggers all wore earbuds, presenting no danger of eavesdropping.

"What really scared Chief Barton," Valkonen told Duarte, "was Justine didn't tell him about this little death concert."

"How'd he find out?"

Valkonen sighed. "I told him."

"You?"

"Justine asked her brother if he'd take her to the show."

Duarte stopped walking, put a restraining hand on Valkonen's arm. He liked the way it felt, even through the sweatshirt.

"You're telling me your chief's daughter is suicidal?"

"She only wanted to go and watch, what she told her brother."

Duarte grimaced. "Oh, well, that's *much* better."

They started walking again. Valkonen missed the feeling of Duarte's hand on him when she let go of his arm.

"Justin came to me for an opinion," he said. "If he and Sis went to the show and didn't kill themselves, did I think there'd be people there who'd kill them for chickening out? Justin's the reader in the family. He knows about Jonestown: how the ones who didn't drink their Kool-Aid got a helping hand."

"I bet he wanted to watch, too."

"Kids," Valkonen said. "Everything's a reality show."

Duarte stopped again, faced the beach and the ocean. A hundred feet below them, traffic zipped up and down the coast highway. A sign near the fence on which Duarte rested her hands said the bluffs were subject to collapse. You entered the park at your own risk.

Valkonen turned his back on the possibility of seismic deconstruction and parked a hip on the fence so he could look at Duarte.

"I told the chief everything Justin told me. He shipped both kids to his sister in Vermont that same afternoon. Which left me in need of a new assignment, and you know what that turned out to be."

Duarte hung her head for a moment, took a deep breath,

and looked at Valkonen. "You think there's any chance this is for real? I know what you said about figuring it out but you've been thinking about it longer than I have. Give me your take."

"I do a bit of reading myself," he said. "I checked out group suicides. They do it in Japan."

"Yeah, but isn't that their culture?"

"Suicide is, but it used to be more of a personal thing. Private. Just the individual and his or her despair. But this multi-party stuff is fairly new. And putting ads on the Internet to have perfect strangers take the jump with you is definitely novel."

"How do they do it?" Duarte asked. "I mean, is there a preferred way? Something that might give us a lead?"

"I don't think so. The demise *du jour* is very low-tech. Asphyxiation." Valkonen gave her the specifics. "Thing is, once people make the commitment, they find it very hard to back out. Like it'd be worse to disappoint some jerkoff than kill yourself."

"Peer group pressure."

"Of the worst kind."

"So it could happen?"

"Yeah, I think so — if the loons involved are organized enough. If they get their logistics right. If we don't find them in time."

"Yeah, and how do we know how much time we have?"

Valkonen told her. "Justine met the kid who gave her the word Saturday, two days ago. He said a week, ten days at the most."

"Probably next Saturday, make the front page of the Sunday *Times*."

"Could be," Valkonen allowed. "Or maybe it's an 'I don't

like Mondays' thing. And we're already too late."

Duarte pushed off the fence, started off in the direction of their cars.

Valkonen gave her a little head start. Checked her out from behind. Caught up before she wised up and clocked him.

"You have any kids?" Duarte asked.

"Yes and no."

She gave him a look, letting him know she didn't go for bullshit.

"I have a kid sister," Valkonen told her. "One of those *oops* babies Mom and Dad never see coming. Anyway, there's a 14 year difference between us, but I've loved Evie heart and soul ever since she came home from the hospital."

"That's terrific, but it's not what I'm asking."

"Wait, I'm getting there. It turns out Evie likes girls as much as I do. More, even, as she actually married one."

Valkonen thought Duarte was going to stop again or maybe put her hand on him once more, but she only gave him a look like she had an idea where he was going. A good sign since they'd be working together.

He told her, "Sergeant Keegan isn't the only one who's gone up to San Francisco to be in a wedding."

Duarte saw now why Valkonen had done Keegan that particular favor.

"Your sister and her partner," she said, "they were in that rush of people who got married up there when the mayor said it was okay."

"I was honored to be their best man," Valkonen said. "I would have been delirious to be the groom once I met Dana."

Duarte nodded. Now she had it.

"So there're these two ladies you have very positive feelings about, and who should they turn to when they need someone to be the sperm donor for their baby?"

They were at their cars now: Valkonen's new Nissan 350Z; Duarte's city-issue sedan. Valkonen took out his wallet and showed Duarte a picture of a little boy about seven, front teeth missing from his wide smile.

"That's Jack," he said. "Evie and Dana used to joke they had to get married so he'd no longer be a bastard. Jack calls me Uncle Rick. We go to ball games. Fish. When Evie and Dana get to feeling secure enough, I'll teach him to surf. If, God forbid, anything ever happened to both Evie and Dana, he'd come to me. If something happens to me, Jack gets everything I have."

"So it's working out okay for all concerned?" Duarte asked.

"Great. Dana's a financial planner. I turned all my money over to her right after she and Evie got together. I'm probably the richest honest cop you'll ever meet."

Duarte gave him a wan smile. She took out a picture of her own. Her boy was maybe eight or nine years older than Jack. As good looking as his mother but with a very serious expression.

"Sebastian. Straight-A honors student. Has Ivy League schools sending him mail already, and his sophomore year isn't even over. But no daddy. No Uncle Rick. Just a mom who tries real hard. Tries not to be *too* hard on him."

"Where's he go to school?" Valkonen asked.

"Santa Monica High. Mom has a great big mortgage on a very small condo in town."

Treading lightly, Valkonen asked, "You don't think he'd—"

"Know about this concert? Go to it? I hope to God not. But you said it yourself: kids."

"How about Sebastian knowing where we might find a lead?"

Duarte put her son's picture away.

"I'm going to ask him. Very carefully."

"You want me along?"

"You can wait outside. I'll call you in if I think it's a good idea."

Valkonen nodded. Duarte gave him her address. Told him to show up fifteen minutes after Sebastian got home from school. He could park at the hydrant out front.

"Okay," he said.

He thought that'd be it until that afternoon. But Duarte had a couple of questions.

"You're not worried about working with me?" she asked.

Meaning, did he think, he got her ticked off, she might file some bogus complaint against him, end his career on a down-note.

"Unh-uh," Valkonen said. "I like working with a cop who packs a punch."

Duarte smiled and asked her other question.

"I don't have a lot of money put aside, but you think your friend Dana might do something with what I've got?"

Valkonen said, "I'll talk to her."

CHAPTER 3

Evie, Dana, and Jack lived in a rambling one story frame house just east of Westwood and just south of Wilshire. The location put the house in an actual Los Angeles neighborhood, not one of the three Bs — Beverly Hills, Bel-Air, Brentwood — that most of America considered movie sets for wretched excess and celebrity homicides. Like any home on the Westside it was priced at a not-so-small fortune. When the doorbell was pressed it played the first four notes of Beethoven's Fifth Symphony.

The homeowners liked every visitor to feel his arrival was momentous.

Evie opened the door dressed in a baggy gray sweatshirt featuring Mickey Mouse wearing a beret and holding a palette and a paint brush — bought at Euro-Disneyland — and a pair of paint-spattered Levis. Her feet were bare.

She stood on tiptoe to kiss Valkonen's cheek.

"My favorite big brother," she said, beaming.

"Your only big brother."

She took his hand, led him inside, and closed the door behind them.

"That's true," Evie said as she led Valkonen through the house, "but I've observed many other people's big brothers and you're the best I've ever seen."

"Will you make me a plaque saying that?"

"Sure, if you want."

They entered Evie's studio at the back of the house. It faced north and sunlight flooded through the skylight and French doors. Outside was a pool that always put Valkonen in mind of a banjo: a circular area for splashing or lolling, bisected by a long, narrow, vertical extension for lap swimming. Steps away from the studio was the house's kitchen, stocked with fresh fruit, veggies, and other nutritionally acceptable munchies. Across the room from Evie's drawing table was an 8-foot long sinfully comfortable leather sofa. It was Valkonen's bed when he stayed over; Evie's resting place when she called it quits after working deep into the night.

Evie was an editorial design consultant for a number of glossy regional magazines around the country. Once when describing her job to Valkonen she'd told him: "I show them how to sculpt their white space."

Valkonen had said, "Uh-huh."

He came to understand what she meant when she showed him a couple examples of her work. He saw how the text you read, the photos you looked at, were greatly affected by how they were framed by the blank areas — white space — around them.

But he wasn't visiting his sister for that. He wanted her to draw a picture for him.

Evie was a killer portraitist. Far more gifted than police sketch artists.

They'd been through the exercise enough times that she'd anticipated the reason for his visit. She perched on the front half of the high, rotating chair at her drawing table. She flipped open a pad of paper, and snagged one of the many finely sharpened pencils she always kept on hand. Valkonen had never seen her sharpen a pencil but she always had a vast supply.

Maybe Dana handled that chore for her.

"Okay, what kind of a villain are we tracking this time?" Evie asked, ready to go.

Valkonen stretched out on the sofa.

"Maybe not a villain at all, maybe just a kid."

"Boy or girl?"

"Boy. About eighteen. Six-one, skinny, maybe one-fifty."

Evie started sketching out a rough body shape: vertical, ectomorphic.

Valkonen recalled the description of the boy Justine had provided, the one who'd passed the word to her about the suicide concert. Both Valkonen and the chief had to drag the specifics of the kid's appearance out of Justine, but they'd gotten everything the girl could remember.

"Face shape, hair?" Evie asked.

"Oval. Bushy."

"African-American?"

"No, white. Not wiry hair, but dense, wavy, no styling at all."

"Color?"

"Dark brown."

"Eyes?"

"Hazel."

"Any distinctive features?"

"Unibrow. Recessive chin. Long sideburns. Blotchy complexion."

"Other features?"

"Just-a-nose nose."

"Not big, hooked or broken?"

"Unh-uh. Mouth's ordinary, too."

Valkonen looked over at his sister as she worked, seeing her from behind. She had long straight pale blonde hair, the kind you saw occasionally on kids, hardly ever on adults. The color was still natural as far as he knew. Her shoulders were square and strong from daily use of the pool outside. Turn her around and her face was more handsome than beautiful, until she smiled, and then it was stunning. When Evie was younger, Valkonen used to think that whoever the guy was who wanted to marry his baby sister would have to meet with his approval. Dana wasn't a guy, but she more than hit the mark.

Made him smile to think how things could work out.

Evie asked, "What kind of clothes?"

"Latter-day acid-head. Brightly colored t-shirt, baggy green twill pants with a lot of pockets, don't know about the shoes."

"I'll put in something appropriate. Do you know anything about his personality."

Valkonen didn't hold back with Evie. He told her about the concert.

The hand holding the pencil faltered momentarily.

"So this boy is suicidal?"

"That or he wants to go to watch. That's a possibility, too."

Evie nodded. "Two kinds of illness; I'll do a likeness for each."

He let her finish her work in silence. She completed her drawings, scanned them into her computer, worked a little software magic to get right and left profiles of her drawings, and a rear view, too. She burned the artwork onto a DVD for him and gave him the disk in a jewel box. Then she finally let her feelings show.

"This is awful, Rick. I hope you can do something."

"Me, too. How're Jack and Dana?"

She gave him her best smile but it faded fast.

"They're great. I'm so happy that sometimes it scares me. I sit back and wonder how long it can last. Now, I'll wonder more than ever. All those kids, could they really..."

"I know. I've got a new partner on this one. We'll both be doing everything we can." But just then an idea entered his mind that he didn't want to voice.

Evie saw his frown and asked, "What is it, Rick?"

"I was just going to ask what kind of music Jack likes these days."

His sister smiled. "He's in second grade. He still enjoys music that Dana and I approve. Peter, Paul and Mary, mostly."

"Okay."

"Dana has a few teenage nieces and nephews. I could have her ask them what groups they like."

"Yeah, do that."

Evie knitted her brow and this time Valkonen bit.

"Okay, what's on *your* mind?"

"I just remembered, Rick. Isn't there a Rolling Stones song with a lyric about suicide onstage?"

"Yeah, I think there is," he said, and smiled . "I just flashed on the L.A. Coliseum filled with 100,000 graying baby-boomers for the Stones' no-shit farewell performance."

Evie laughed. "That is funny, considering your generation wants to live forever."

"Thank God someone does."

"It's Only Rock 'n' Roll." Valkonen remembered the Stones song with the onstage suicide reference — Mick singing about sticking a knife in his heart — as he drove over to Detective Joan Duarte's condo. He thought about her name for a moment: Joan. He'd never met a Latina with that name before. If they got to know each other better, he'd have to ask her about it.

Duarte's condo might have been small but it was on a good block just off Colorado and it was in a nicely designed building. He could imagine that even a place of modest square-footage at that address went for a blockbuster price; you left your windows open, you'd feel ocean breezes. He wondered if his new partner's mortgage was subsidized by the city. In Santa Monica, such things were possible.

Thinking of Duarte's finances as he pulled into a legal parking space, just up the street from her building, he remembered that he hadn't asked Evie if Dana was taking on any new clients — per Duarte's request. He shut down his engine and called Evie.

"Hey, Sis, it's me. I forgot to —"

Maybe sixty feet away Sebastian Duarte, Valkonen was pretty sure, came out the front door of the condo building, his face not just serious but tight with teenage anger.

"Hold on, Evie," Valkonen said, "I've got a situation here. Nothing dangerous, just ..."

Sebastian had a new haircut, not the conservative style in

the photo his mother carried, but something with a lot more attitude: the top as flat as the flight-deck of an aircraft carrier with a spiked point up front. The boy looked up and down the street and Valkonen was sure now he was looking at Duarte's son.

Sebastian's gaze swept over Valkonen but he wasn't looking for someone sitting in a car. The cop doubted he'd registered in the kid's consciousness at all. Then Sebastian smiled and waved. He took off jogging, heading west as Valkonen watched over his steering wheel.

"Rick, are you still there?" Evie asked.

Valkonen saw Sebastian heading in the direction of a blonde girl.

"I'm here, Evie. You at your drawing table?"

"Yeah."

"Can you do a quick sketch for me?"

"Sure, go ahead."

He concentrated on the girl first.

"Young woman, fifteen to twenty, blonde." He squinted, thought he saw dark roots. "Bottle blonde. Straight shoulder length hair, parted down the middle." Sebastian had reached her by now. They held hands. The girl looked to be a couple inches shorter than the boy; he'd peg Sebastian at maybe five-nine. "Height five-seven, weight one twenty-five. Pale orange crop-top. Faded flared blue jeans. And ... flip-flops on her feet."

The girl seemed underdressed for a cool day, he thought. Sebastian must have felt the same way; he put an arm around her shoulder and the two of them walked west.

"Bust?" Evie asked.

"No, no arrest."

"Not you. The girl. Her bust."

"Oh. Maybe a B-cup." Another detail popped into his head. "She had something in her navel, some kind of piercing. I couldn't see what it was."

"Rounded belly or flat?"

"Flat."

"Anything else?"

Valkonen hesitated. He wasn't sure how his new partner would take it if he had a drawing done of her son. Hell, there might be no reason to have a drawing of the girl, for that matter. It was just ... well, he knew that Duarte had said she was going to talk to Sebastian about the suicide concert, and not long after that conversation should have taken place the kid came storming out of his home, looking plenty pissed.

The cop in Valkonen said it would be a good idea to have a likeness of the girl Sebastian had gone off with.

"Rick," Evie said, "Dana just brought Jack home from school. You need me any more?"

"No, Sis. Thanks a lot. Give them my love."

"You'll stop by for the drawing of this girl?"

"Absolutely."

They said goodbye just as Duarte came out of her building. She looked up and down the block, too. Unlike her son, she spotted Valkonen sitting in his car. He opened the door and got out.

He had an awkward choice to make. Admit what he'd seen or deny it. Building trust with his new partner inclined him to be candid with her. Being sensitive to her family problems, maybe he should say he'd arrived that very moment.

He'd have to see if she felt like throwing one of her punches before he decided.

CHAPTER 4

Valkonen opted for misdirection and asked the approaching Duarte, "You have a computer that can print from a DVD?"

She took a look in the direction her son had gone.

Valkonen wondered if she'd seen Sebastian go that way from a window or simply had an idea where he might be heading. He wondered, too, if had Duarte seen the blonde girl.

She turned to look at him.

"Yeah, I've got a computer that can do that. You've got something?"

Valkonen held up the jewel box.

"Maybe our first lead."

"Let's go take a look."

She turned, quickly walked to her building, and pushed through the front door. He had to catch up before the door closed on him.

There was an elevator opposite the front entrance but Duarte opened a side door off the reception area and ran up three flights of stairs. Valkonen was close behind, admiring the athletic ease with which Duarte moved. Some of that energy was coming from anger but a lot of the spring in her step was the product of well-toned muscle, which he found reassuring.

His attitude toward working with a woman was far more enlightened than most of his brethren in blue, but he'd admit to himself that his preference in a female partner was someone who could complete a triathlon.

Duarte sped down the hall to her condo and got the door open quickly. That was when it finally penetrated Valkonen's consciousness that she was trying to get inside before he had a chance to see something. She might have asked him to give her a minute before coming up, but being pissed off and all ... well, he was learning a thing or two about her.

He slowed his pursuit. Gave her a couple of beats to hide anything she didn't want him to see. But he didn't make his dawdling so obvious he'd have to explain he'd caught on.

When he got to the open door, he cleared his throat to announce himself. She called out to him from someplace off to his left. "You want anything to drink?"

"Whatever you've got." He looked around.

Just inside the door to Duarte's condo were a coat closet on one side of a small entryway and opposite it a mirror with a shelf for keys or a purse. Or, being a cop, a gun and a sap. Whatever you needed before going out. He closed the door behind him.

Ahead to his right was a short corridor with three doors: two bedrooms and a bathroom, he guessed. Ahead was the living room/dining area with windows that looked out on the street, the space maybe 200 square feet.

"Cranapple juice, okay?" Duarte asked.

The kitchen was tucked into a corner off the dining area.

"That's fine," he said.

"Ice?"

"Straight."

The furniture, Valkonen saw, looked comfortable and clean but not new. What caught his eye was the open laptop computer on a coffee table. That and the art on the wall. Original oils, all of them done by the same artist, if he had it right. Vividly colored palmy paradises in the style of Rousseau. The French artist had populated his works with nude women and tigers battling buffalos, but these paintings were more informed by the music of Guns 'n' Roses: L.A. as a jungle filled with urban perils.

Duarte handed Valkonen his glass of juice.

She'd seen him studying the paintings and told him, "My brother's work."

"Yeah?"

She nodded, sipped her drink through compressed lips. She stared at a painting of a tropical forest. Among the trees stood a lightpole with a street sign saying Hollywood Boulevard. Peering from the shadows and behind shrubs were junkies, whores, pimps, and muggers. They were costumed in breechcloths, White Sox caps, and spiked heels.

Valkonen found the painting to be both disturbing and humorous.

And well done.

Duarte seemed to regard it with anger. But if she chose to hang it in her home, the problem wasn't with the art but the artist. Family problems.

Ones that involved Sebastian? That'd be his guess.

Duarte sat on the sofa and put coasters on the coffee table for their drinks.

"Have a seat," she told Valkonen.

He sat beside her, leaving a foot of open space between them

"Let's see what you have." She extended her hand for the jewel box.

He passed it to her. She opened the box and popped out the DVD. Slid it into her computer. The machine's screen showed a desktop of files and applications. Valkonen was sure that something else had been on the monitor before he'd entered Duarte's home. There was nothing else in the place she could have tidied up so fast. Duarte certainly hadn't gotten so pissed off at Sebastian because he'd failed to make his bed or had left dirty dishes in the kitchen sink.

Which left the computer. And maybe some nasty site sonny-boy had been visiting?

Duarte clicked on the icon for the DVD and the likeness of the kid they needed to find popped up on the screen. Valkonen told her who it was and how he and the chief had wrung the description out of Justine.

"Wow," Duarte said, clicking through the renderings of their subject. "This should be a big help." She hit the print command and Valkonen heard a printer go to work in the area where he'd guessed the bedrooms were. "Whole building's Wi-Fi," she said.

Valkonen nodded. "Nice."

Duarte continued to look through the renderings of their target on her computer, imprinting the images in her memory. "You've got some great sketch people at LAPD."

Valkonen shook his head.

"I've got an artist in the family, too."

She looked at him and made the leap.

"Your sister?"

"Yeah."

Duarte said, "I like her work better than Eugene's."

Valkonen didn't say a word. Only met Duarte's gaze.

She'd just confirmed his assumption: the problem she was having involved both her son and her brother. Now the question was could she — would she — share it with a guy she'd met just that morning. If he'd been anyone but another cop, and her new partner, she probably wouldn't have said a word.

As it was, she tapped her keyboard and a picture appeared on the screen: Sebastian and the blonde girl Valkonen had seen with him. Only this time they were naked. Standing side by side, each with an arm around the other's shoulders — and a hand covering each other's crotch. They were on a beach somewhere, the ocean blue and choppy behind them.

Valkonen took it in for a few seconds and turned to his new partner. Waited for her to speak.

"He was supposed to be at my brother's house in San Diego," she said. "Spring break trip to visit the artist uncle, learn a little about painting. See if he might like it."

The cop in Valkonen supplied some of the details.

"Which was just a dodge," he said. "Your boy brought his girlfriend along and they went to that nude beach down in San Diego."

"Ha!" Duarte said. "Can't screw on Black's Beach. They went to Mexico! With a thousand other damn young fools taking all their clothes off. Most of the others, though, looked like they were in college. You know, 18 or older. Legal fornicators."

Valkonen sighed. "So two underage kids crossed the border, in both directions, had to be using phony IDs. And nobody saw through their con."

Duarte nodded. "Some goddamn homeland security, huh?"

"And your brother didn't rat them out."

Duarte blanked the screen with a finger jab that would have put an eye out.

"He thought it was funny. And when I started yelling at him he got oh so calm and logical: '*Hermana*, a boy has to become a man sometime, and this was with a girl he loves, a girl who loves him. I made Sebi take condoms. Where is the harm?'"

She looked at Valkonen almost daring him to agree with her brother. Or even say *kids* again. He declined on both counts.

Duarte continued, "Then my dear son has the nerve to put his smut on my computer so he can make a movie out of it. There's much more than you saw. He didn't think I'd find the file he created. This is my *work* computer. What if somebody — and I've got more than one enemy, believe me — found this filth? I'd be arrested for child pornography!"

For a moment, she looked like she was going to fling her glass of juice against a wall featuring three more of her brother's paintings, but she restrained herself.

"It was *so* stupid," she said, "but I ... I didn't handle things well at all."

Valkonen commiserated. "Tough situation. I might have raised my voice myself."

"I did more than that. I told him I didn't want him to ever bring that girl home."

"Ouch."

"Yeah. Then I fired the other barrel. I told him I was going to call the girl's parents so they'd know to keep my sex-crazed son away from their daughter."

Valkonen nodded, thinking that would get the boy pissed off, all right. Scare the hell out of his girlfriend, too. Make her wet her pants thinking what her parents might do.

His new partner, Valkonen now understood, was someone you wouldn't want anywhere near the launch button for a nuclear missile.

Duarte laughed, almost as if she could read his mind and had found the thought funny, but there was more self-recrimination in her voice than humor.

"You know what else made me crazy?" she asked. "That goddamn new haircut of his. Such a *punk* haircut, and he has such beautiful hair. I thought maybe it was just an impulsive thing. He'd let it grow out and that'd be that. But when I saw his smutty pictures I got it, what it really is. It's his I'm-a-man-now haircut. He's going to stand up to me from now on. He even said so. Right before he ran out the door."

Clearly, Duarte thought that was pretty punk, too.

Valkonen decided he didn't need to ask whether Duarte had gotten any information from Sebastian that might help their investigation. The mood she was in, she probably favored adolescent suicides.

He said, "You need a day or two, I'll start looking for the kid we want by myself."

In the blink of an eye, she was on her feet glaring at him.

"Like hell you will. We're in this together. This kid was working *my* town."

Valkonen stood up, too. Nice and easy. No challenge implicit in the move.

"Okay. Glad you're up for it. But one thing."

"What?"

Her eyes still held a lot of anger that was looking for a way out.

"We get lucky," he said, "find this kid sooner rather than later, and you're still pissed off, I'm going to be the one who questions him."

She started to say something, probably something unpleasant, but she held back, clenched her jaw. Understanding they were both working a punishment job already and further fuckups — like beating the hell out of a person of interest — would not be tolerated, she finally nodded.

But she said, "Just hope you don't have to put up with shit like this when your little guy gets older."

Exactly what Valkonen was thinking.

Putting Duarte's wayward son aside for the moment, the two cops discussed their next move and quickly decided they needed help. Duarte hadn't been a regular in the live-music scene since 1990. She didn't have to say why; Valkonen did the arithmetic. That was when she got pregnant. Valkonen was even farther removed from club music; he hadn't seen anything other than stadium shows since David Crosby's first drug bust.

But, interestingly, they both listened to NPR, specifically KDSW right there in Santa Monica. The public radio station was renowned for its commitment to airing new music, from alt-rock, to reggae, to world music, to anything they thought was worth a listen.

Valkonen and Duarte went out and got into his car for the short drive to the radio station. On the way, Valkonen admitted to his new partner that he tuned in to KDSW mostly for its news programming.

"Far as music goes," he said, "I still like the stuff I grew up with."

"Don't write 'em like that anymore, huh?" Duarte asked, still cranky.

Valkonen didn't take offense.

"No they don't," he said. "Wish to hell they did. The old guys, I can understand, they've fried their brain or blown out their eardrums, and just can't do it anymore. But, damn, hasn't anyone in the current generation been influenced by them?"

"Maybe Bush'll bring back the draft," Duarte said. "Get all that righteous, revolutionary anger going again."

"That could do it."

Valkonen pulled to a stop at the end of a long line of cars. The light ahead was green but nobody was moving.

"Can you see what the problem is?" Duarte asked, craning her neck.

Valkonen shook his head.

"Hate to need an ambulance or fire truck right now," Duarte said.

It was only four o'clock and traffic was already grid-locked.

"Or even a cop," Valkonen replied.

They looked at one another, saw they were thinking the same thing. No way in the world was either of them going to exit the car and flash a badge just to try to get traffic moving. For one thing, it was likely beyond their power to accomplish. For another, a cop tried that when it wasn't his job might get put back on traffic detail permanently. Such was the humor of police bosses.

But times like this, when a street was paralyzed for no apparent reason, tended to make people crazy, and in any sizable number of motorists at least a few would be carrying weapons in their vehicles. *They* might be tempted to wade into the intersection to get things going.

That happened, Valkonen and Duarte would have no choice but to intervene. Which might result in a firefight in the thick of the afternoon commute. It hadn't happened yet, but speculation that it would was a hot topic of discussion among local law enforcement agencies.

"You see that poll in the *Times* the other day?" Valkonen asked.

"Which one?"

"The one that said one of every three people living in L.A. seriously wants to leave town in the next five years."

The two cops looked at each other and, just like they'd rehearsed it, both of them said, "Fine with me."

They laughed, Duarte's mood lightened, and all the motorists around them managed to divert themselves from homicidal impulses. Everybody, perhaps inured to life in the city, just chilled.

Duarte asked, "You an actual L.A. native?"

"Yeah, third generation. You?"

"Second generation. You going to Blue Heaven when you retire?"

Meaning Oregon, Idaho, or Montana, where a lot of burnt out SoCal cops went.

"Nah. I told Dana my investment goal is to buy a place, no matter how small or humble, on the ocean in either L.A. or Orange counties."

"Wow! She can help you do that, she must be good. You ask about me?"

"Left a message." A lie. Valkonen had now forgotten twice about Duarte's request, but would correct the situation as soon as he could.

"You get your place, can I come visit?" Duarte asked.

"Bring burgers and beer, you'll always be welcome."

"Deal." Duarte paused a minute, then asked, "Something like this concert, a thousand kids really killing themselves ... you think that'd get the traffic in this town to thin out faster?"

Valkonen gave her a look and said, "Silver lining to every cloud."

They both laughed again.

Then he added. "But we still have to do our jobs."

"Yeah."

And for no apparent reason traffic began to move again.

They got to the radio station, went inside, and asked to speak with Ian MacShane, the music director.

Nonplussed by the arrival of two cops, the receptionist could only think to ask, "Well, are you both contributing members of KDSW?"

Turned out, they both were.

CHAPTER 5

Ian MacShane came across as a British Dick Clark, a guy who'd been around since Elvis first sang "Hound Dog" and hadn't aged a day since. His office reflected the station policy of bringing new music to the public. Posters, one-sheets, and handbills of groups Valkonen had never heard of covered most of the wall space, everything tastefully framed and artfully lighted, of course. Valkonen looked at Duarte and raised an eyebrow at her. She nodded in the direction of one poster. Both cops frowned. *Weezer?*

Which confirmed they needed help. Between them, they were maybe 1 percent aware of what kids liked to listen to today. Valkonen was glad for the familiarity of seeing MacShane in a black-and-white photo with the Stones on the credenza behind his desk. Guy looked exactly the same then and now; only the '60s suit he wore in the picture, and

Mick and Keith looking like teenagers, gave away the passage of time.

MacShane had them take the guest chairs opposite his desk and opened his arms wide. "How may I help?"

Duarte started as they were in her town.

"We might be facing a very serious situation, Mr. MacShane."

"Please. Call me Ian."

"Thank you, Ian. Before I get into substance, I have to ask that you keep our talk confidential."

"Does it have anything to do with the station?"

"No. We're here because we need ... expert guidance."

"Very well. Mum's the word."

Duarte trusted the man, but looked at Valkonen to get his take. He nodded. She told MacShane the story. He listened without interruption. Didn't say the whole thing was preposterous. In fact, the expression in his eyes grew more thoughtful, and for the first time he began to look like the 60-something scholar of contemporary music he was.

Valkonen slid a copy of Evie's sketch onto MacShane's desk: the mystery kid.

"He's the one we're looking for," Valkonen said. "Maybe he was just blowing smoke, trying to impress a girl with an outrageous story. But that's not the feeling Detective Duarte and I get from it."

MacShane picked up the portrait and examined it closely for several seconds.

Looking up, he said, "Nor do I. The most famous case of music-inspired suicide, of course, is the one where a young man killed himself and his family sued Ozzy Osbourne, blaming his song "Suicide Solution" for the death. The family lost the suit, but there have been other instances where popular music—"

"Rock 'n' roll," Duarte clarified.

"Well, yes." MacShane shrugged. "Who would kill himself whilst listening to disco?"

"Me," Valkonen said, "if it went on too long."

"Quite," MacShane agreed. "Now that you raise other possibilities, I can think of several blues songs that might accompany one to the Great Beyond."

Duarte nodded. "Sure, after you've *lived* the blues at least at a little. But we're talking kids here, too dumb to know their troubles don't amount to much."

"Yes, well, that's a subjective judgment, isn't it?" MacShane asked. "But I agree we're probably talking rock. Pop is too bright and sunny. Metal would fit more neatly with a homicidal rage than a suicidal leap. You should be looking, I think, for a nihilistic snarl. Punk, in a word. Three ragged chords on guitar, a bass line urging haste, and the drums hammering like a heart racing toward its last beat. The lyrics might say anything, of course, but in the end what they'll amount to is a surly fuck you."

MacShane had been talking to Duarte and Valkonen, but his eyes had been looking inward. When he stopped speaking, he gave no sign he was aware his visitors were still present.

"Ian," Duarte said. "*Ian.*"

The music director bestirred himself.

"Oh, my, I am sorry. How rude of me."

Valkonen understood where MacShane's reverie had carried him.

He told the man, "You've been there, close to the edge."

"Close enough to *see* the edge anyway ... and to remember the sense that the only affirmative choice left was to select the moment and manner of one's own demise."

Duarte asked quietly, "You got some help, right Ian?"

He laughed, dispelling his momentary gloom.

"Did better than that. I married my therapist. Now I get my head shrunk for free." He opened a desk drawer, took out a business card, and handed it to Duarte. "My wife's office number. I'll let her know we've spoken, in case you might want some insight keener than an old music man might offer."

"Thank you, Ian," Duarte said.

"There is one thing that puzzles me," MacShane said.

"What's that?" Valkonen asked.

"The underlying premise. A large group of people won't turn out to see just any band, much less kill themselves at a stranger's behest. So what's the hook?"

Duarte turned to Valkonen. The expression on her face said that she should have thought to ask that question or, having failed to, Valkonen should have covered that ground.

Which he did, apologizing first to his new partner.

"Sorry. Should have mentioned those details. This band supposedly had an underground monster hit with their first album. The likes of which they could never hope to equal."

MacShane understood immediately. "The only way left to go is down, unless they—"

"Pull the plug altogether," Duarte finished.

"Yeah," Valkonen said. "As for the audience—"

"They'll see the concert of their lives," MacShane said.

Valkonen added, "The crowd, the music, the hysteria. If you feel your life is shit going in, it beats sticking your head in an oven."

MacShane nodded, his face grave once more. "That might have been enough to ..."

He didn't finish his thought. He didn't have to. Both cops could see the mature, polished professional in front of them imagine the time when he would have been front row center at the death concert, ending his days in a way pop culture was sure to immortalize.

He abruptly stood up and announced, "I must make a phone call. You don't have any idea of this band's name, do you?"

Valkonen and Duarte also got to their feet.

"No," Valkonen said. "No name on the band or the kid in the drawing."

"May I keep the sketch?" MacShane asked.

"Sure. We've got more."

"Ian, you going to be okay?" Duarte asked.

He nodded absently and told them he knew people at every level of the music business. He'd do everything he could to help them. He even gave them a suggestion as to what they might do next.

When Valkonen and Duarte got back to Valkonen's car, she asked him, "Ian's going to call his wife, right? Get some help."

"Hope so," Valkonen said. "We're supposed to prevent suicide, not drive people to it."

Valkonen and Duarte drove into Los Angeles, heading for the Sunset Strip, but it was too early to see the guy whose name Ian MacShane had given to them. So they fought traffic only as far as the Hamburger Hamlet on Sepulveda. The restaurant chain had pared its numbers way back from what it had been in the old days but the Hamlet still served great burgers and mountainous slabs of devil's food cake. They got a booth, gave the waitress their orders, and Duarte excused herself to use the ladies room.

When she came out, she used the pay phone. Valkonen noticed because he paid attention to his surroundings, but he made it a point not to watch his new partner make her call. Couldn't stop the cop-thoughts from running through his head, though. He was certain that Duarte, a detective, carried a cell phone. She'd no more leave it at home than forget her badge or gun. Wanting privacy, she should have used the cell to place her call from inside the women's john. But something had prevented that. Low battery or poor signal reception maybe. So she'd come out and used the public phone.

To call Sebastian, no doubt. Try to get past her anger and show her concern. That or tear her son a new one.

The waitress brought their orders and a moment later Duarte slipped back into the booth. She saw that Valkonen hadn't touched his food.

"You didn't have to wait for me to start eating," she said.

"I try for the occasional moment of grace."

Duarte smiled thinly. "Makes you pretty rare around this town."

Valkonen raised his glass of club soda to her. Duarte clinked her glass of iced tea against it.

"Happy endings," he toasted.

"Yeah, we should be so lucky."

Valkonen sipped his drink and then applied himself to his burger. It was big enough to give a vegan nightmares, and he tore almost a quarter of it off with his first bite. Duarte stared at him as he masticated. Valkonen smiled at her, cheeks distended.

Swallowing, he said, "Yum."

"You can't always eat like that," she told him. "You wouldn't look the way you do."

"How's that?"

"Smaller than an Escalade."

"Stop, you'll turn my head."

"Okay, you're more like that Z you drive," she said.

"Spoken like a true Angelena. I'm surprised *your* dinner is enough to keep you from fainting away with hunger."

Duarte had ordered a turkey breast sandwich on whole wheat with a few sprouts thrown in so she'd have something to stick to her teeth if not to her ribs.

"If I had anything more," she told him, "I'd look like my *abuelita*."

She wasn't going to look like anyone's granny any time soon, Valkonen knew. Her temper probably burned more calories daily than most people's workouts. But he wasn't going to argue the point. They were just dancing around things, getting to know each other.

"So've you ever been married or what?" Duarte asked.

"Or what," Valkonen answered.

He closed in on his burger again, wiped a squirt of mustard off the corner of his mouth. Duarte addressed her healthful, calorie-conscious sandwich. She took a smaller bite than he did but she chewed harder.

Wouldn't do to have Duarte sink her teeth into you, he thought.

"I was married," she said. "Almost a year."

"Longer than some," he replied.

"My ex left because he was afraid of me."

"Yeah? You give him reason?"

"We got back from our honeymoon in Hawaii, I told him if he ever cheated on me I'd kill him."

"You suspected something that soon?"

"I didn't like the way he was looking at some of the women on the beach over there. That was when thong bikinis first started appearing in big numbers. He checked out a few too many of those *wahines'* backsides to suit me."

"That's all?" Valkonen asked.

"Well, he's a carpenter on movie shoots, too. You know how movie people are."

Valkonen didn't, not personally, but he was curious about something else.

"At the time you made your threat —"

"You don't have to say it like that."

"Okay. At the time you *warned* your new husband, were you already a sworn officer, carrying a badge and a gun and all that?"

"Yeah, I was. That was one of the things he liked about me, the way I looked in my uniform."

Poor sap probably conjured a fantasy or ten about Duarte in her uniform, Valkonen thought, but doubtless he hadn't figured on receiving a death threat from his new bride.

"Anyway," she continued, "I was still in the hospital after giving birth when he came to me and said he hadn't cheated on me but we had to get divorced. Said I'd scared him so badly his hair was falling out. It was getting thin real fast and it wasn't a flattering look, so I gave him his divorce. Never saw him again after that day in court, but his child-support check is always right on time, first of every month."

"Is there any man you haven't scared?" Valkonen asked.

"You seem to be holding your own," Duarte said. "You going to tell me about your 'or what' or not?"

"I lived with a woman, another LAPD cop, for nine years."

"You can do that? No rules or regs against it?"

"It's neither encouraged nor discouraged. The exception is where two cops are in a direct chain of command, one superior, the other subordinate. Then there are rules. But we weren't in that situation."

"So what happened," Duarte asked, "one of you cheat?"

"If you mean with other people, no."

"What other kind of cheating is there?"

"Well, there's the academic kind. See, when Penny and I met we were both patrol officers, and we both passed the sergeant's exam at the same time. As long as we kept our ranks in sync, everything was fine. Problem was, we both wanted to keep on climbing the ladder. She made lieutenant and I didn't."

"And you think she cheated somehow?" Duarte asked.

"I had to help her study for the sergeant's test. She didn't have a bad mind, but she needed lots of repetition for things to sink in. But for the lieutenant's exam she brushed off my offer to help. Said she felt confident she'd do well."

"Did she?"

"Aced the test. Without studying at all, as far as I could tell."

"How'd you do?"

"Top score among white males."

Duarte sneered. "Meaning top score period."

"No. Sergeant Byron Yang edged me by two points."

"Get back to Penny."

"She was promoted."

"And you think she cheated?"

"She'd started taking ginkgo biloba capsules around that time, but I don't think that explains the increase in brain power," Valkonen said.

"So somebody put in the fix?"

Valkonen shrugged, took another big bite of his burger.

Duarte asked, "Why would somebody want to do that for her if she wasn't sleeping with him? You said she wasn't cheating on you."

Valkonen washed down the burger with a slug of water. "She wasn't. There was no time for it. We spent all our usual time together."

"Did you resent her promotion when you didn't get yours?"

"I wasn't happy about my situation, being discriminated against."

"Yeah, that's a bitch, isn't it?"

Valkonen ignored the sarcasm. "I tried to be happy for her."

"So what was the problem?"

"I didn't say a word, but Penny could tell I was wondering how she'd passed her exam. It became this thing between us, an unspoken irritant. Little bad habits we used to let slide became daily arguments ... and of course a lieutenant couldn't take any lip from a mere sergeant. Got to the point where I had to leave before things got violent.

"Me leaving, that was okay with her," Valkonen continued. "What wasn't okay was when I asked for my half of the equity in the house we'd bought together. That was when Penny sued me for palimony."

Duarte looked at Valkonen in disbelief. "*Palimony?*"

"Yeah, like I was a movie star or something. Hell, with her promotion, she was making more money than I was."

"I can't believe I didn't read about this in the paper."

Valkonen said, "The suit never got that far. My sister got me this bulldog female lawyer. She told Penny she was going to find out for sure how Penny got her promotion, see whether there was anything hinky about it. That's when the suit got dropped, the house got sold, I got my half of the equity, and Penny paid my legal fees."

Now, Duarte's eyes gleamed. "You got her good. She can't even come back at you or your lawyer goes right back at her with the same threat."

Valkonen said, "Things worked out for her anyway. She's a captain now. Married to a retired deputy chief. Lives in a much nicer house than the one we had."

"Damn! He was the one who helped her cheat on that test — and she was glad to see you go because she had Big Boy waiting in the wings."

Valkonen finished his burger and water.

"Come on," he said, "let's get the check and get going."

Duarte wrapped the half of her sandwich she hadn't eaten in a napkin, and didn't object when Valkonen picked up the tab.

Traffic had thinned and the sun was close to setting when they got back to his car.

Duarte told him, "Sebastian wasn't home when I called. He had his cell turned off, too."

Valkonen looked at her.

"You worried? You want to go home?"

"Yes ... and no," Duarte told him.

CHAPTER 6

Even having stopped for dinner and the getting-to-know-you conversation, it was still early as Valkonen and Duarte cruised east out of Beverly Hills and onto the Sunset Strip. Their eyes tracked the string of clubs where the music wouldn't start for a couple more hours. They passed the Whiskey, the Roxy, the Viper Room. Duarte nodded her head at that last venue.

"That's where River Phoenix collapsed and died," she said.

"Unh-huh," Valkonen agreed, from behind the wheel.

"Johnny Depp owns the place."

"Yeah."

"You don't like him? Johnny Depp?"

"Loved him in *Pirates of the Caribbean*. The first one."

Duarte said, "Yeah. You know, a lot of big rock bands

came out of these clubs over the years. Must be kind of intimidating for new acts. Try to think they have the stuff to fill all those big shoes."

Valkonen glanced over at her and grinned.

"Testosterone and pharmaceuticals, they'll get you past a lot of inhibitions."

"Keep the likes of you and me on the job, too."

They found a parking spot just up the street from a new club called Clive's. Rumor had it the place was named after a legendary star-maker in the music business. The mogul didn't confirm that story, but he hadn't had his lawyer send a cease-and-desist letter to the club's management either.

Meant the man really did own the club or at least he was okay with the joke. That was the popular interpretation, anyway. And the place seemed to have the biggest names in rock drop in for impromptu sets on an almost weekly basis.

The other thing it was known for was giving good new bands the chance to show what they could do. That was why Ian MacShane had sent Valkonen and Duarte there.

Valkonen knocked on the locked front door, gave it a minute and knocked again.

"You ever kick a door?" Duarte asked.

Valkonen shook his head.

"Never shot a gun out of a bad guy's hand either."

Duarte gave him a dirty look.

"*I* kicked a door once," she said.

"Hurt your knee?"

"My ankle. Never did it again. I just wanted to know about you, you know."

A guy Valkonen recognized as a former offensive lineman from USC and the San Diego Chargers opened the door.

"We don't open for another hour," he said politely.

The two cops showed their badges.

"Ian MacShane at KDSW sent us," Duarte told him. "We're here to see Mickey T."

The big guy smiled warmly and waved them inside, locking the door behind them.

"Yeah, I got the word on that. I just didn't register you as cops, the body language between you or somethin'." He shrugged. "I'm Walter Thornberry."

He shook hands with both Valkonen and Duarte.

"How about I take you back to Mickey's office and bring you something to drink?"

"You work the door, Walter?" Valkonen asked.

"The door, inside security. Little bit of everything."

"You have many underage kids trying to get inside."

Walter nodded. "Enough. I'm real good at spotting fake IDs."

Valkonen took out a copy of the picture of the kid they were trying to find.

"You ever see him?"

Walter studied the drawing and his brow knitted.

"You have seen him," Duarte said.

"Yeah, I think I have. But not here."

"Where?" Valkonen asked.

"That's what I'm trying to remember."

Duarte leaned forward but Valkonen put a hand on her arm, holding her back.

"Let me give you my card, Walter. You remember, you call me, okay?"

"Absolutely."

He took them back to the general manager's office. The space was small, windowless, and the walls were covered with posters of rock shows dating back fifteen years. The oldest were from Bloomington, Indiana: campus shows at the university. Others were from clubs in Chicago. The venues switched to the east coast the closer they came to the present. Boston, Providence, and New York.

The guy they'd come to meet was seated behind an old wooden desk, looked like it might have belonged to a third-grade teacher at one time. He leaned forward, listening intently to whomever he had on the phone, but divided his attention enough to gesture to his visitors to take the guest chairs opposite him.

"Good," Mickey T said into his phone and hung up without another word. He looked at Valkonen and Duarte and smiled. "Michael Telephus, pleased to meet you."

He stood long enough to shake their hands.

The two cops shared the same thought: Mickey T didn't look old enough to get past his own doorman. The impression was heightened by the Indiana University letter-sweater he was wearing.

"You mind me asking," Valkonen said, "what your sport was?"

Mickey T said, "Fencing. Epée in competition. Sabers with some friends. Now that I'm out here , I'm studying kendo."

"You any good?" Duarte asked.

"Had a spot on the Olympic team until I separated my shoulder in a traffic accident."

"Must've been hard, losing that kind of opportunity," Valkonen said.

"Yeah. Especially when the other driver was drunk. But that was a long time ago. Ian called and asked if I could be of help to you. Didn't say more than that, kept it kind of mysterious. Made me curious."

"We're hoping you might have some demo CDs from groups looking to play your club," Duarte told him.

Mickey T laughed.

"You bring your U-Haul with you? What's the name of the group you want to hear?"

"Well, that's the problem," Valkonen said. He explained that they didn't know the name. All they knew was the group was probably punk-rock and they'd put together an exceptionally solid collection of songs for their first album.

"Yeah?" Mickey T's interest was piqued. "Sounds like the kind of band we like around here. Normally, I'd be able to give you my top ten, the bands we intend to book in the near future, have people from the big labels here to take a listen. But I was away for the last month, wrapping up some business back east."

"How many new demos do you get in a month?" Duarte asked.

"Maybe five hundred. Bands from all over the world want to play here."

Valkonen asked, "You do any scouting? Just to make sure you're not missing anything good?"

Mickey T looked at him with a new interest.

"Yeah, we do."

"Because, funny as it might seem," Valkonen said, "this group we're looking for might not be interested in a recording deal."

"That would be *very* funny. Unheard of, in fact," Mickey T replied. "But kids do pass a lot of Garage Band CDs back and forth among themselves. I suppose it's possible a group would be satisfied with that level of audience. But usually real talent wants the widest possible exposure."

"And the most money?" Duarte asked.

"Goes without saying. But ..." Mickey T drifted away for a moment.

"But what?" Valkonen asked.

"Well, a lot of these young musicians grew up watching *Behind the Music*. They know a shit-storm of hassle is part of the package when you get famous. Maybe these guys simply want to avoid all that." Micky T grinned. "Wouldn't that be interesting?"

"Yeah, art for its own sake," Duarte said.

"Positively subversive," Valkonen added. "Put you businessmen in a real bind."

"I'm not going to lose sleep anytime soon," Mickey T said with a smile. "Is there anything more you can tell me?"

"Not right now," Valkonen said.

"How about you give us the name of some places where you scout new bands?" Duarte asked.

"Sure, how big a net do you want to cast? Regionally, nationally, globally?"

"Locally will do to start," Duarte answered.

Mickey T gave them a name. And said he'd have all the demos he had on hand copied.

They could pick them up tomorrow morning.

Mickey T sent Valkonen and Duarte to a place in the Valley called Sapphire, an all-age club. It didn't sell alcohol so any kid who could get his parents' permission, or just sneak out of the house with five bucks in his pocket, could gain admission. Mickey T said it was the kind of place commonly known as an earplug club.

He gave each cop a pair of cellophane-wrapped earplugs.

Valkonen and Duarte thought Mickey T was joking with

them until they got out of the Z a half-block up Sherman Way from Sapphire. The music coming from the club was loud at that distance. Sapphire's neighbors were a grab-bag of retail store fronts, dark for the night. Nobody around to complain about all the racket.

"Jesus, they must all be going deaf in there," Duarte said.

"Unless they're wearing their earplugs," Valkonen replied.

"Probably blast their iPods just as loud," the angry mom detective told him.

Valkonen began to wonder if Duarte's son had been an *oops* baby.

The two of them approached the club. It was a nondescript stucco structure lit from the outside with blue lights. A navy blue canopy extended from the front entrance. The club's tinted windows bounced in their frames in time with the music.

Outside were two valets, who looked barely old enough to drive, conversing in animated sign language.

Valkonen and Duarte looked at each.

"You know how to sign?" he shouted at her.

She shook her head.

He shrugged, went over to the closer of the two valets, a dark-haired kid who combed it back in a '50s-style pompadour. Valkonen even thought he smelled Brylcreem. Had a hard time believing the stuff was still being made. Maybe it was just another thing that had escaped his notice. He showed his badge to the kid and pointed to Duarte.

She had hers out, too.

A gleaming red '64 Mustang pulled to a stop in front of the club. The other valet opened the passenger door for a girl Valkonen thought could be no more than twelve — if you looked at her face. Lower your gaze, you had to wonder how young you could be and still get your breasts augmented. That and get a charge account at Frederick's of Hollywood. The driver, by contrast, wore a Dodger's cap on backward, a UCLA basketball jersey over bony shoulders, baggy green pants he had to hold up with one hand, and enormous orange sneakers.

The driver tipped the valet ten bucks.

The two young club-goers didn't give Valkonen and Duarte a second glance as they passed by. The doorman greeted them like celebrities, which for all the two cops knew they were. Once the new arrivals were inside, the guy on the door came over to see what the old folks at the curb wanted.

He was tall and wiry, maybe mid-20s, which probably qualified him for the senior's discount at Sapphire. He had some wear and tear on him, too. His knuckles were scarred and he had prison tattoos peeking above the collar of his ripped T-shirt. An edgy guy to impress the hell out of the pre-pubes.

"You lookin' for your kid?" he asked Valkonen and Duarte at a shout. "Tell me his name. I'll bing him out for you."

The cops brought their badges out once more, along with the picture of the boy they sought. Valkonen said loudly, "This is who we want but we don't know his name."

The doorman gave the drawing a glance. Moved closer to the cops so he wouldn't have to bellow at the top of his lungs.

"Me neither. Never saw him before."

He gestured to the slick-haired valet, deftly signing, apparently asking him to look at the sketch. He did but he shook his head, too.

"Billy don't know him either."

He shrugged and started back toward the door.

"Hey," Duarte yelled.

The doorman stopped, stepped back.

"Yeah?"

"Who's the responsible adult in there? And there damn well better be one."

"Got a retired cop. That suit you?"

"He's running the place?" Duarte asked.

"Unh-uh. That'd be Vass."

"Vass?"

"Vassily Baklanov. You want to see him, you can go around back. His office has a door right off the parking lot."

"Yeah, thanks," Duarte said. "We'll just use the front door."

They did, Valkonen donning his earplugs as they went inside.

Valkonen could see the band on the stage at the back of the room: four guys who looked like they came out of the same cell-block as the guy on the door. Only not dressed quite so nicely. Their T-shirts and jeans were shredded to such an extent they looked liked they'd been stripped from the victims of a car-bombing.

The music inside the club was so loud that Valkonen could feel the fillings in his teeth vibrate. He'd have to send Mickey T a thank you note for the earplugs. He looked to his right at Duarte. She wasn't using the plugs; she had her index fingers stuck in her ears. She was having a hard time seeing the band. Most of the kids in front of her were as tall as she was, and dancing had apparently evolved into jumping up and down in place, which ruined Duarte's view.

Valkonen suspected obstructed sight lines had little to do with the look of disapproval on his new partner's face. Doubtless, she'd like to blister the bottoms of every little reprobate in the room. Before she could act on that impulse, Valkonen caught her eye and nodded to a pair of doors on their left. They headed that way.

The doors looked like they belonged on a restaurant kitchen: swinging stainless steel with black rubber bumpers and a circular pane of glass in each one. The two cops pushed through — and were immediately relieved by how the decibel level dropped. Duarte took her fingers out of her ears; Valkonen removed his earplugs.

The two cops looked around them.

The room was a long rectangle with a battered hardwood floor and light provided by a half dozen antique neon signs for brands of cigarettes. Someone had sprayed a sardonic caveat against the dangers of tobacco on the back wall in neon-green paint: *Smoking kills. So does everything else.* The room was filled with a higgledy-piggledy arrangement of Salvation Army sofas and easy chairs. Occupying the second-hand furniture were teenage couples, and a few threesomes, giving vigorous expression to their hormones.

Having recent experience with an offspring engaging in such behavior, Duarte muttered, "Jesus Christ, what are we coming to?"

Valkonen didn't know but he saw someone who might be better equipped to offer an opinion. He said to his partner, "Over there."

She followed his gaze to a huge brown man who sat on a high barstool in a far corner of the room. He was looking back at them but didn't get off his perch. The mountain not coming to them, they went to the mountain.

"Kimo Arenui," he introduced himself. "Used to be a desk sergeant in Hollywood. Where you guys work?"

Letting them know he knew they were cops; no need to see their badges.

Valkonen and Duarte told him who they were.

"You lookin' for some kid, right?"

They nodded. Valkonen showed the sketch. Arenui studied it closely, ran the image against the database in his head. And nodded.

"Yeah. This boy's been here."

The two cops got excited.

"Tonight?" Duarte asked.

"Do you know his name?" Valkonen added.

"If he's here, he's in the music room." Arenui nodded toward the metal doors, a distasteful look on his face. It was no coincidence he was seated as far as possible from the din. "Can't help you with the name, never heard it."

The two cops looked at each other, silently arriving at a division of labor. Valkonen put her earplugs back in and went to the outer room to look for the kid they wanted. Duarte knew she owed him one.

She asked Arenui, "What's your job here, sergeant?"

"Enforce the rules."

"The rules being?"

"No drugs, no booze, no fighting, no fucking, no oral copulation."

"Regular Romper Room you're running here."

"Pretty much."

Duarte made a sweeping gesture at the young crowd, all of whom were too preoccupied to notice her. "You approve of all this?"

Arenui sighed. "You got your own kids giving you problems, don't you, Detective?"

Duarte didn't answer.

"Look," Arenui said, "I come from a culture where people start early. With sex, I mean. But then we don't think it's shameful. Never have. Well, some of us do, women mostly, been away from home too long. But what you got here is kids not using drugs, getting drunk, driving drunk, killing each other, having intercourse, or transmitting sexual diseases. But they *think* they're getting away with murder. So they keep coming back — instead of going places they could really mess themselves up."

"And nobody ever dares breaks your rules, that what you're telling me?"

Arenui smiled and said, "Watch."

Without making a show about it, he stood up. Which took him to at least six-and-a-half feet tall. Made Duarte, standing next to him, look like a pre-schooler. Every young head in the room disengaged itself and turned toward him.

Arenui held up a benevolent hand, almost as if blessing the young people, and settled himself back on his stool. A moment later adrenaline levels retreated and the adolescent crowd returned to their explorations of self and other.

"Everybody who comes here knows," Arenui told Duarte, "I put you out, you stay out."

She thought about that. Looked over her shoulder. No Valkonen.

"I ask you something that stays just between us, Sarge?"

"Sure."

She took out her picture of Sebastian, showed it to him.

"This boy comes in, he's got a new buzzcut, you let me know?"

She gave him a business card with her home number on

the back. Arenui put it in his pocket and nodded.

"Want me to hold on to him till you get here?"

Duarte nodded.

"Yeah. You call me, I'll get here fast."

Arenui bobbed his head and said, "Here comes your LAPD guy."

Valkonen rejoined them. "Didn't see him but, honest to God, I think that music's loud enough to make you blind."

"Does me, I get too close," Arenui agreed.

"We'd like to see your boss," Valkonen told him.

"Be fine, only he's not here. Left maybe ten minutes before you arrived. He doesn't get out of his office much anyway. Just handles the money, booking the bands, business stuff. Wouldn't know one kid from another."

"But you say he hires the bands?"

"Yeah."

"You hear any group lately that sounds a whole lot better than most?"

Arenui laughed. Sounded like a volcano getting ready to blow.

"Man, they all sound the same. Like shit."

"Well, just in case one comes in that does sound better, give me a call, okay?" Valkonen gave Arenui his card.

"You got it," the big man said. Then he asked, "I see the kid you're looking for again, you want I should sit on him for you?"

"With both cheeks, Sarge."

CHAPTER 7

Valkonen and Duarte returned to the Sunset Strip, spent hours walking up and down the sidewalk, stopping into clubs and restaurants, even badging their way into private clubs, all to find the kid who'd told Chief Barton's daughter about the suicide concert.

That and maybe luck out and find the band that would headline the gig.

But if it wasn't for bad luck they wouldn't have had any luck at all.

Best thing that could be said, the last stop they made, Valkonen liked the band onstage, an outfit called Multiport. Two guys, two women. Guitars, bass, and drums. All of them could play; all of them could sing; and somebody was writing actual rock 'n' roll songs for them. It was enough to give Valkonen hope for the future.

He sat at the bar, sipped a beer, and listened raptly. Duarte was paying back the debt she'd incurred at Sapphire by interviewing the club's manager and security people, then going the extra mile by letting her new partner soak up the music until the band finished its set.

Driving Duarte back to her condo, Valkonen said, "Can't remember the last time I was at a club till closing time."

"You gonna ask me what I found out?" Duarte asked.

"Sorry. What'd you find out?"

"Not a damn thing. Nobody knew nothing. But you were having a good time. Lost yourself way deep in the music."

"Yeah, I did, didn't I?"

They were both silent for a moment, thinking about that.

"If you can get that swept up —" Duarte started.

"Think how easy a crowd of kids could be carried away," Valkonen finished.

He glanced over at Duarte, saw a look of concern etching lines in her face.

Didn't feel he knew her well enough to start talking about her son.

She'd have to open that can of worms.

Instead, she surprised him. "You touched me tonight."

"What?" He didn't know what she was talking about.

"In Clive's. With that doorman, Walter. I wanted to press him on where he thought he saw that kid we want. But you held me back. Put your hand on my arm."

Now he remembered — that and something else.

"Yeah, I did. But you set the precedent this morning in Palisades Park. You caught hold of *my* arm, remember?"

She did, her eyes widening, and her mouth following in a yawn.

Duarte rubbed tired eyes and said, "Yeah, we better

watch it."

"You made me think of something, mentioning Walter just now."

"What's that?"

"He and the sarge out at Sapphire both recognized our kid."

"We gotta give him a name, this kid," Duarte told Valkonen. "Make him more real. Easier to refer to."

"Waldo."

Tired as she was, Duarte managed to laugh.

"Yeah, right. Where's Waldo?"

"Anyway, Walter and the sarge both recognizing Waldo, maybe they had to cool him out ... at their clubs or somewhere else. Like maybe he has an attitude. Or a temper."

Duarte saw where Valkonen was going.

"Maybe Waldo's come to the attention of the kiddie coppers, L.A. or SMPD."

"Unh-huh."

"So we pass along our wonderful sketches, see if we can't find out Waldo's real name."

Valkonen nodded, but Duarte could see that he had something else on his mind.

"What?" she asked.

"Just something else I was wondering, not about the case."

"What?"

"Well, I never met a Latina named Joan before. Wouldn't have been nosy enough to ask for the story behind it, but your relentless interrogation just now broke me down."

Duarte snorted.

"It was my dad's idea. Mom wanted to call me Yoana. They both mean the same thing but Dad wanted my name to be American so I could fit in better."

Valkonen didn't go anywhere near that one, but he asked, "What do they both names mean?"

"God's gift."

Another opportunity to crack wise, but he didn't.

Only said, "Perfect sentiment for any child, boy or girl."

Valkonen pulled up in front of Duarte's building. He hadn't meant for his comment to lead into a discussion of his partner's kid, but hearing what he'd said she might ...

Sidestep that topic neatly.

"You know that band you liked tonight, Multiport?" Duarte asked

"Yeah?"

"You ever think they might be the ones we want?"

"Unh-uh. They were anything but suicidal. They were into their music and each other. Blind man could see that."

"You got that right. Club manager told me, far as he knows, they're the first band that's entirely bisexual. Everybody's getting it on with everyone else."

Valkonen grinned. "Explains their name. Still like their sound."

"Yeah," Duarte said and opened her door. "Good night, Sarge."

"See you bright and early, Detective."

He watched her enter the building.

There were no lights on in her unit.

Meaning her kid was asleep ... or he'd never come home.

CHAPTER 8

Tuesday

A soft hand stroked Valkonen's cheek. Once, twice, and once more.

Then a throaty contralto voice told him, "That's all you get, you're awake."

"Is it time for school already, Mom?" Valkonen asked, eyes still closed.

"Yes, and you haven't done your homework."

Valkonen opened his eyes. Saw his sister's beautiful black-haired, green-eyed spouse, Dana.

"Marry me," he said.

"That'd be bigamy."

"Big of you, great for me."

Dana smiled and said, "Sit up, flatfoot."

He stretched and yawned first, then complied. He'd stopped in at his sister's house late last night because it was closer than going home; because he wanted to pick up Evie's sketch of Sebastian Duarte's girlfriend; but most of all because he wanted to see Jack sleeping peacefully, not yet touched by all the dark things the world might send his way far too soon.

After he'd satisfied himself on that count, without waking Evie or Dana, he'd locked his gun in the house's safe, kicked off his shoes and fallen asleep in his clothes on the wonderful sofa in Evie's studio. He'd expected she'd be the one to wake him up, not Dana.

Who sat down beside him and put an arm around his shoulders.

"I'm winning you over?" he asked.

"You already have my heart. Well, half of it. It's the rest of me you can't have."

"I'll have to become a tragic poet when I stop being a cop."

"I thought you were going to be an overaged surfer."

"That, too. How's my money doing?"

"Very nicely. You should be able to afford a *two-room* beach shack."

"Indoor plumbing?"

"Let's not get greedy."

Dana removed her arm from Valkonen's shoulders and took his right hand in both of hers, looked him right in the eye.

"Uh-oh," Valkonen said. "Did I do something bad or forget to do something good?"

"Neither. It's what you need to do. Talk with Jack."

"About?"

"About where he got his Y-chromosome. He had a class in school yesterday. Got him to wondering who his daddy is."

They'd all known this day would come, but none of them had expected it would come so soon — the curse of a progressive private school education.

"Did you and Evie tell him?"

"We asked who he'd like it to be, if it could be anyone."

"And?"

"Jack said you or Bill Nye the Science Guy."

Valkonen grinned. "Well, if I rate with a celebrity ..."

"He'll be here in a minute. We told him he'd meet his dad. Try not to take it too hard if he's expecting Bill."

Now, Valkonen hugged Dana and felt her shiver.

"Don't worry," he said, "Jack loves you and Evie more than anyone."

"Except you."

Both Evie and Dana worried how their relationship with Jack might change once he learned who his father was. Valkonen always reassured them that while it might be different it wouldn't be diminished. And he did so again.

"*I* love you and Evie more than anyone, too," he said.

"Except Jack."

"Yeah."

Dana kissed Valkonen's cheek as gently as she'd stroked it earlier — just as Evie walked in with their son.

"Dad?" Jack asked, looking at Valkonen.

He didn't seem disappointed at all.

Jack's moms left him alone with his father. The boy sat as close to Valkonen as Dana had. This time it was Valkonen who lightly placed his arm around his companion's shoulders. Jack looked up at him and immediately sought to clarify their relationship.

"So you're my Uncle Rick and my dad, both?"

"Exactly," Valkonen said.

"Well ... does that kinda thing happen a lot?"

"More than it used to, but it's still pretty new."

"But how should I think of you? What should I call you?" the boy wanted to know.

"I hope you'll always think of me as someone who loves you very much. What you call me is up to you. Maybe you should call me Dad on Father's Day and Uncle Rick on Uncle's Day."

Jack giggled. "There's no such thing as Uncle's Day."

"Give Hallmark a little time. Here's what you do: think it over, what you'd like to call me, talk to Evie and Dana about it, and whatever you three decide is okay by me. That fair?"

Jack's head bobbed in agreement.

"Can I come live at your house some of the time?" he asked.

Shared custody. Definitely not part of the agreement Valkonen had worked out with Evie and Dana. Something he'd never even considered before. But now that Jack had brought up the idea it held a certain appeal. Especially after he stopped being a cop and had a lot of time on his hands.

But still being a cop, he was suspicious of even his son's motives. He asked, "Do you mean, maybe, you'd like to come live with me the times you're mad at Evie or Dana?"

Caught, Jack lowered his eyes and nodded.

"Being mad at someone's hard, isn't it?"

"Yeah."

"But making up is pretty special."

Jack grinned. "Yeah, I usually get an ice cream soda."

"That's a much better deal than I offer. When I make up with someone I give them a glass of onion juice."

Jack scrunched his face into a credible impression of a gargoyle.

Then he said, "There are still times I'd like to be with you. Mommy Evie and Mommy Dana, when I want to play catch, they throw like girls, and they're complete spazzes when they try to catch the ball."

"Hmm," Valkonen sympathized. "You know, that's only going to get worse. Because the bigger you get, the harder you'll throw, and we wouldn't want them to get hurt by accident."

Jack shook his head; injuring his mothers was definitely a bad idea.

"How about this? Whenever you're feeling, let's say, manly, we'll all get together and work out a time when you can come over to my house and we'll do some manly stuff."

Jack's eyes got big. "Yeah."

"But remember, one of the big things about moms?"

"What?"

"You can't be away from them too long because they miss their children something awful." Valkonen let his face go long, turned down the corners of his mouth, and carried on in a tremulous voice. "Stay away too long and their hearts start breaking; they just sit around the house all day and wail."

Valkonen knuckled his eyes and went boo-hoo-hoo.

Jack laughed and pounced on him.

"You can't cry, silly, you're a policeman."

He was reminded of that fact just then as Evie and Dana appeared in the doorway, the two of them looking horrified.

Evie said, "Rick, give Jack to Dana and come into the kitchen quick."

CHAPTER 9

The television in the kitchen showed one of L.A.'s end-less supply of supermodel-newswomen standing on a beach under an overcast sky. The caption under the picture ID'ed the reporter and the beach: Allison Smyth and Leo Carrillo.

"The body of the nude young woman, estimated to be in her mid-teens, was found early this morning by two fisher-men. There were no signs of physical trauma and the coro-ner's office won't release a cause of death until an autopsy is performed. But unofficially authorities consider the death to be a drowning. Whether it occurred as an accident or a sui-cide, they can't say ..."

Terrible, Valkonen thought, but he didn't understand why Evie and Dana were taking the matter so personally. He turned to look at Evie but she told him to keep watch-ing the tube.

"Once again," Ms. Smyth said, "here is a picture of the victim."

The shot of the reporter on the beach was replaced by a still photo of the dead girl's face, the reporter's voice continuing in voice-over.

"No clothing or identification was found on the beach in the immediate area of where the body washed ashore. Authorities are asking anyone recognizing this person to call —"

Valkonen turned the TV off. He knew all the numbers to call.

"Rick," Evie said, "is that the girl you described to me over the phone yesterday?"

He nodded. "Sure is."

Sebastian Duarte's girlfriend.

Valkonen showered, changed into fresh clothes he kept at Evie's house, kissed everyone goodbye, and carried a Tupperware bowl of fruit salad to his car, where his cell phone rang.

"Valkonen," he said, sliding behind the steering wheel.

"It's me," a raspy female voice responded.

"Joan?" He hadn't known her long enough to be sure.

"Yeah."

She sounded like hell.

"I saw the story on the tube," he said. "Sebastian?"

"Fate unknown."

"So no body," Valkonen said. "Are you on the scene?"

"Yeah. Audra's parents called me at three this morning. I was up anyway. Mrs. Stevens asked if Audra was at my place, and if she wasn't could I please get the cops to start looking for her because she had this real bad feeling."

"Oh, man."

"Yeah. Shit." For a long moment Duarte was silent.

Valkonen said, "Joan?"

She continued her story. "I called a friend on dispatch at SMPD, had him put out the word to all the local departments. Sheriff's unit responded to the call from the fishermen this morning. The word got back to me. I drove up here, made the ID ... called Audra's parents."

Who were now being allowed the trivial solace of making funeral arrangements for their daughter in privacy while the cops misled the media into thinking the victim hadn't been identified.

Other details had also been held back.

"The two fishermen who found Audra were a couple of older guys. Apparently, they hadn't seen much bad stuff in their lives. Just made their call and ran back to their car to wait for the sheriff's unit. Didn't notice that the body had been posed."

"Posed how?" Valkonen asked.

"Hands covering pubic area, hair pulled forward to cover the breasts."

Duarte's words formed a picture in Valkonen's mind; the image was much like the photo of Sebastian and Audra on the beach in Mexico.

Duarte continued, "The sheriff's detectives are pretty good. They've already turned up someone who remembered seeing Audra walking along the beach yesterday at sunset. She was holding hands with a thin dark-haired boy with a buzz cut. Might have been Latino."

"Oh, God."

"Yeah. The grouper troopers say it's perfectly possible for

one body to wash ashore and another to go out to sea and vanish forever."

"But what about the posing of Audra's body?" Valkonen asked.

"Somebody showed her a little respect, yeah. Doesn't mean it had to be Sebi."

Valkonen couldn't think of one hopeful thing to say. You couldn't bullshit a cop.

So he asked a cop question, "Someone watching your condo while you're at the beach? In case Sebastian did make it and goes home."

"Yeah, I have a couple friends left at SMPD."

"What about Eugene?" Duarte's artist brother in San Diego. "Think Sebi might head down to his place?"

Duarte was silent; she hadn't thought of that.

When she found her voice, she said, "I'm glad one of us is still thinking like a cop. I'll make the call right away."

But she didn't; instead, she asked Valkonen three questions.

"If Sebi is alive, why didn't he do the right thing? Why didn't he call 911 himself?"

And with her voice breaking, "Goddamnit, if he's alive, why didn't he call me?"

Valkonen was a *pro re nata* — as need arises — Christian. He murmured brief words of supplication for the deliverance of Duarte's son. As much as he'd have liked to be with his new partner, he knew that he had no standing in the matter, and his hunch was that Duarte was not the type, even now, to take kindly to having her hand held.

He decided the best thing he could do was get on with

his case.

See if he could spare other parents the prospect of losing their children.

He got the sketches of Waldo to the Youth Services office of the LAPD. Explained that he was working a job directly for the chief and would appreciate the prompt distribution of copies of Waldo's image to every division in the city — and to have copies sent to SMPD. If any officer in either city knew Waldo's identity, Valkonen wanted to hear right away.

Having invoked the chief's personal interest, he was sure his request for help wouldn't languish in the bureaucracy.

He drove from downtown to the Sunset Strip. The traffic heading west was relatively light. Here and there, in hotel restaurants and a few trendy diners, producers, writers, agents, and other show biz fauna were trying to put together deals over scrambled egg-whites and decaf but, by and large, the early daylight hours were quiet and the sidewalks stood all but empty.

Which made it easy for Valkonen to spot Walter Thornberry sitting on a barstool outside of Clive's reading the morning paper. Next to the security man were two large cardboard boxes, each of which bore the logo of Cristal champagne.

Valkonen pulled up opposite Walter and got out of his car.

"Morning, Walter," Valkonen said.

"Hey, Sergeant." Walter stood up, put his paper down on the stool. "You want to open the back of your car, I'll load these boxes for you."

Valkonen popped the release and watched Walter pick up the first box. The effort didn't make the big man grunt or strain, but the weight was enough to make the muscles in Walter's arms stand out in sharp relief. Made the back end of Valkonen's Z sit lower when both boxes rested on the rear deck.

Closing the car's back end, Valkonen asked, "Those're all demo CDs in there?"

Walter nodded.

"You count how many there are?"

Walter grinned. "Not a productive use of my time, you ask me. Mickey T did say, though, there were too many to spend money duplicating. So you get the originals. He asks that you kindly return them when you're done. In good condition, just in case there's one or two it'd be worth his while to hear."

"You need a receipt?" Valkonen asked.

"Man's word should be his bond. You gonna bring all them things back?"

"Yes."

"Works for me."

"What do you think of most of the music you hear in there, Walter?" Valkonen nodded in the direction of Clive's.

Walter smiled again. "It puts me in mind of what I used to hear from my coaches at the end of my football career: I appreciate your efforts but not your results."

Valkonen laughed and asked, "So why do you do this job?"

"I'm learning the club business. Have one of my own someday. With music *I* like."

"You think of where you saw that kid in the picture I showed you?"

Walter shook his head. "It'll come to me, though."

Valkonen hoped it'd come sooner rather than later.

"Did have one idea," Walter said. "A maybe 'bout where I

saw him."

"Yeah?"

"Well, you know how bands plaster their names and the places they're gonna play on light-poles and bus stops and all that. Usually, it's guys in the bands themselves do that, but sometimes they got a few bucks to spare, they hire kids to do it for them. Maybe that's where I saw the kid you want. Doin' that kinda stuff. Don't know for sure, but it'll come clear."

"Yeah, thanks, Walter."

Valkonen shook the big man's hand.

He got into his car. Cruised slowly up and down Sunset checking out all the homemade handbills and posters that had been affixed to every imaginable surface. Copied down all the names and dates and venues of where bands would be playing. Or had played, as nobody ever took down old publicity efforts.

He dropped down to Santa Monica Boulevard and did the same thing for a few blocks to either side of the Troubadour.

By the time he was done it was lunch time and he had the names of 68 bands.

None of which he'd ever heard of.

CHAPTER 10

Valkonen had a laptop computer that played CDs, but he'd heard a tech cop talking one time how home-made discs were as likely to carry viruses as a streetwalker, and until somebody invented condoms for computers you didn't want to stick bad plastic into your PC. The warning was graphic enough that Valkonen didn't even want to take the demo discs home and play them on his stereo system.

Might be biological viruses on the damn things, too, for all he knew.

He stopped at a discount electronics store and bought the cheapest Walkman knockoff he could find. Kept the receipt. Either the department would reimburse him or the accountant Dana used would figure a way to write the purchase off as a business expense.

Valkonen set up shop in Roxbury Park, a quiet green

nook south of Olympic, across the street from the campus of Beverly Hills High School. Central American nannies hovered over the offspring of rich Anglos in the park's playground. They ignored the man sitting at the shaded picnic table wearing surgical gloves and taking CDs from a big box.

The gloves were to avoid adding his fingerprints to any that might be on the discs. That and shield him from cooties.

From the jumble in the box, Valkonen plucked ten CDs and constructed a neat stack. He opened his notepad and wrote down the names of the bands and the order in which he would listen to them:

1) Cancer Ward
2) Dogpile
3) Spastic Colon
4) Dragging Muffler
5) Comé Mierda
6) Bestiary
7) Dreadnought
8) Fool's Errand
9) Innermost Circle of Hell
10) Adverse Reaction

He looked at the list. Wondered if anybody in the first group had ever suffered from the Big C or read Solzhenitsyn. Wondered if anybody in group nine thought life was hell or had read Dante. Wondered whether group two had inspired group five to tell people to eat shit. Wondered whether group ten caused the problem suffered by group three. Wondered most of all if his case wasn't summed up by group eight's name.

He compared all ten band names to the list of groups he'd compiled from the handbills and fliers that were posted on the streets near the music clubs. No matches.

Unable to put it off any longer, Valkonen put the first CD into his new player and began to listen to what passed for music these days. He quickly came to consider it a plus if what he heard didn't actually make his head throb.

He'd gone through three stacks of ten discs, barely making a dent in the first box, when the cops came to his rescue. Beverly Hills cops, older white guy, younger Asian woman, both patrol officers. Drury and Chen according to their name tags.

Drury made Valkonen as a fellow copper, as indicated by a nod of recognition. He gestured for Valkonen to remove his headphones.

"Thank you, Officer," Valkonen said, complying with Drury's directive.

"Who you with, LAPD or the sheriff's department?"

"L.A."

"See your badge?"

"Absolutely." Valkonen produced his badge wallet and opened it.

Both Beverly Hills cops leaned forward for a better look.

"What're you working on here, Sergeant Valkonen?" Drury asked.

He nodded at the CDs.

Valkonen told them he was looking for a kid and a rock group, names unknown, adding, "Hope you don't mind me using one of your parks. I was driving by and it looked like a peaceful place to work."

"No problem. You got a sketch of this kid you want?"

Valkonen took a drawing of Waldo out of his work folio.

Drury shook his head, as did Chen. Neither cop knew the kid.

"You copy this to our department?" Drury asked.

"No, didn't think to."

"How come?"

"Well ... the last pop group to come out of Beverly Hills was Dino, Desi and Billy."

Drury grinned; Chen was too young to get the reference.

"They were from Bel-Air, I believe," Drury informed Valkonen. "Maybe Brentwood."

He turned to Officer Chen and told her he'd be safe without backup. Why didn't she go reassure the complainant everything was okay.

"Neighbor?" Valkonen asked after Chen had left. A row of condo buildings bordered the park.

"Old guy used to be a muckety-muck with the IRS. He likes to keep an eye on the park. Uses these great big binoculars. Saw you wearing gloves, wondered why."

Valkonen took off his surgical gloves. He'd have to find someone to help him listen to the CDs. He did it all himself, his brain would turn to chutney. Wouldn't be able to find his way through a revolving door.

Drury looked at Waldo's likeness again.

"I think you're right," he told Valkonen. "This kid doesn't look like one of ours."

"Would've been too easy. You walk right up and solve things for me."

"Well, maybe I can offer some help. My boy used to be in a band."

"Yeah?"

"Yeah. We live in Hawthorne. You know who came from Hawthorne?"

Valkonen knew, but didn't say. Didn't spoil things.

"The Beach Boys," Drury said.

"Great group."

"Damn right. Anyway, my boy's group was Angry at the World."

"That their name or their attitude?"

"Both," Drury said. "Things might've gone bad for him except he met the right girl. She straightened him right up when his mom and I couldn't."

"Good for her." Valkonen knew that wasn't the point of the story.

"The other guys in the band did get into trouble, after my boy quit. And you know who the biggest asshole of all was?"

"No."

"Their manager," Drury said. "And you know where he lived?"

Valkonen took a guess. "Beverly Hills?"

"Exactly. So you see my point?"

Valkonen wasn't sure.

"What I'm saying," Drury told him, "this kid you're looking for, this band you're looking for, they might not live here but maybe their manager does. Couldn't hurt to put our department into the loop."

Valkonen had never worried about turf or who got credit for what. Probably another reason why he was still a sergeant. He slid a copy of the likeness of Waldo over to Drury.

"Glad to have any help I can get," he said. "But from what I've heard, it's unlikely the group I want even has a manager."

Drury laughed at that.

"Hey, trust me. Any four guys who know three chords and have been together more than a week, they've got a manager. And a groupie and a hanger-on."

"Yeah?" Valkonen asked.

Drury told him, "It's all part of the pipe-dream."

CHAPTER 11

Although cleared to continue his work by the BHPD, Valkonen decided to pack up the demo CDs and move on. The complaining neighbor might be momentarily pacified, but Valkonen had the feeling that someone else was continuing to watch him.

Or maybe listening to bands like The Brain Weevils was making him paranoid.

Heading back to his car, he realized he wasn't qualified to judge what sounds kids today might like. Stuff he considered crap they might regard as bliss. It was possible he could hear the CD from the group he wanted and never know it.

That happened and a lot of kids died, it'd be tough to live with.

But he'd met someone recently who might offer a learned opinion.

He got into his car and was reaching for his cell phone when it rang. He tensed, thinking it might be Duarte with news that her son's body had been found. He found the moment apt to utter another brief prayer.

Which was answered insofar as the woman calling him wasn't Duarte. Her voice carried a slight Germanic accent.

"May I speak with Sergeant Richard Valkonen, please?"

"Speaking."

"Sergeant Valkonen, my name is Marta Waldman."

A name he'd never heard before.

"How may I help you, Ms. Waldman?"

"I ... You visited my husband yesterday, Ian MacShane."

"Yes, I did. With Detective Duarte of the SMPD. I was just—"

"I tried to reach Detective Duarte before I called you but she's not at her office and she has her cell phone turned off."

That didn't sound good to Valkonen. "Detective Duarte is experiencing something of a family crisis right now."

There was a moment of silence and when Marta Waldman spoke again there was a tremor in her voice. "I'm afraid I am, too."

"How's that, Ms. Waldman?" Valkonen asked, growing uneasy.

"Ian didn't come home last night and ..." She was working hard to maintain her composure. "And he missed his broadcast this morning. He didn't even call the station to let them know he wouldn't be in."

Valkonen could imagine people at KDSW scrambling to fill the air-time.

"Has anything like this ever happened to Mr. MacShane before?"

"Never. Ian is a consummate professional."

"Where do you and your husband live?"

"In Santa Monica."

"Ms. Waldman, you should call the Santa Monica police."

With those words, Valkonen told her all her fears were well founded.

Then, changing his mind, he said, "But before you do that, I'd like to talk with you."

Valkonen said he would call the SMPD for her after they spoke.

"I'd appreciate that very much, Sergeant."

He got Marta Waldman's address and told her he'd be there in fifteen minutes.

But before she let him go she said, "I interrupted you a moment ago. That was rude of me. Do you remember what you wanted to say?"

It took Valkonen a moment to recall.

"Yes, I was going to say I wanted to see your husband again. Ask if he might lend me a hand with a problem I'm facing."

"I'd be happy to help, if I'm able."

Always good to distract yourself from your fear, Valkonen knew. But to his ear Marta Waldman didn't sound like someone who'd be plugged into the underground music scene. When he explained what he needed, she agreed.

"Oh, no. I'd be of no help with that. But my grandson, he'd be just the one."

Valkonen said he'd be there as soon as possible.

Duarte was waiting in her car in front of the MacShane-Waldman residence in Santa Monica Canyon when

Valkonen pulled up across the street. She got out of her car first, walked over to Valkonen as he exited the Z. Her face was tight with anger.

Which Valkonen took as preferable to sagging with grief.

"There's a new problem?" he asked.

"Yeah, I almost punched out another cop."

Valkonen gestured Duarte to the passenger side of his car. When both of them were inside, he waited to hear Duarte's story. It wasn't long in coming.

"I just got interrogated."

"What? Who did that?"

"I told you the sheriff's dicks were pretty smart. Well, that stops with their goddamn boss. This asshole lieutenant named Gelb. Fucking blonde crewcut Nazi."

"He have a swastika armband and the high black boots?" Valkonen asked.

Not the response Duarte was expecting. She turned toward the door as if she was going to get out of the car. But leaving without a word wasn't her style. She turned back.

And Valkonen told her, "I was with you at asshole; you lost me at Nazi. My mom and dad had some cousins back in the old country who died at the hands of real Nazis. Bothers me when garden-variety jerks are referred to as actual monsters."

Whatever Duarte had been about to say underwent a quick revision.

"Asshole then, okay?"

"Yeah." By that time Valkonen was able to make the leap, what had Duarte so pissed off. "Gelb was trying blame your son for the girl's death?"

Duarte nodded, her jaw clamped tight.

"What'd he say?" Valkonen asked.

Duarte folded her arms across her chest. "Said he'd talked with the Stevens, Audra's parents. They told him Sebi had their daughter under his control. Like my son is some kind of adolescent Charlie Manson. Gelb asks me did Sebi have other girlfriends, and what are their names? Did he have any Mexican sweeties or was he partial to white meat? How about break-ups? Could he leave a girl, or have her leave him, without things getting violent?"

"Implying Sebi might drown some girl he was done with," Valkonen said.

"Yeah. I told him Audra was the only girlfriend Sebi ever had. He loved her more than he loved me. He has no history of any kind of violence. Go and check himself, if he wanted to waste his time. He sees that's all I'm going to give him, so he hands me his card. Says call him right away if I see or hear from Sebi. I don't, I'll have trouble. More than I had last time. Meaning, he checked me out."

A guy like that, Valkonen thought, he'd be tempted to clock him, too.

"So you responded by ..." Valkonen asked.

"I crumpled his card and tossed it. Into a trash can so they couldn't get me for littering. I walked off toward my car. I heard him start after me. Must not have liked me showing him up in front of his detectives. But after a couple steps he stopped. I think he knew what would've happened, he put a hand on me, tried to turn me around."

"You get a chance to talk to Eugene?" Valkonen asked.

Duarte nodded.

"First time I ever heard my big brother sound less than cocky."

"He hadn't heard from Sebi?"

"No."

"Sorry to hear it."

Valkonen brought Duarte up to date on what he'd been doing. She was surprised by the content of his discussion with Marta Waldman.

"She didn't tell me about that. I called in for messages, got one, all it said was she'd like to talk with me. That's why I'm here. I was trying to get myself under control when you showed up."

A shudder ran through Duarte.

"It can't be a coincidence, us talking to MacShane and him disappearing."

"No way," Valkonen said.

The two cops got out of the car.

Before Valkonen and Duarte could reach Marta Waldman's front door, she appeared at a gate to the right of her tidy gray frame house. She was a short woman with dark hair. The lines on her face said she was somewhere in her 60s; the lines of her body, in a cotton top and linen shorts, said she was a lifelong athlete.

"Sergeant Valkonen?" she said. Glancing at Duarte, she made a second correct identification, "Detective Duarte?"

Valkonen nodded. Duarte said, "Yes, ma'am."

"Won't you please come this way?" She opened the gate for them. "I found it easier to wait for you outside."

They followed her along a flower-lined pathway beside the house, Valkonen closing the gate behind him. There was a terrace and a green space at the back of the house. The yard was small, but someone with an eye for landscaping had made the most of it. Trees sheltered the area from view of the neighbors' houses; three beds of flowers provided a symphony of color; the grass was green and thick but wouldn't take more than five minutes to mow.

Marta Waldman took a seat at a glass-topped, umbrella-shaded table with four padded chairs. On the table were a pitcher of lemonade, three glasses, and a manila file folder. Their hostess gestured to Valkonen and Duarte to sit down. Instinctively, they sat to her right and left, flanking their interview subject.

Marta didn't ask if they'd care for a drink; she simply poured the lemonade and extended a glass to each of them. Neither cop declined her courtesy.

"Where shall we begin?" she asked them. "Other than to say I'm trying very hard not to let you see how worried I am about Ian."

Valkonen and Duarte looked at her, both thinking she was doing a good but not perfect job of hiding her concern. They looked at each other and without a word agreed that Duarte would take the lead in questioning Marta Waldman.

"When was the last time you had contact with your husband, Ms. Waldman?" Duarte asked.

Before answering the question, Marta said, "Would you mind creating a record of our conversation, Detective? That way, perhaps, I won't need to repeat myself to other police personnel."

Valkonen went to his car and returned with a mini-corder. He turned it on, noted the time, location, parties present and had Marta acknowledge that the recording was being made at her request.

Then Marta answered Duarte's question. "I spoke to Ian last night at 6:30."

"For any particular reason?"

"We enjoy conversing with each other. He asked how my

ankle was feeling, and he told me he wanted to prowl the music scene a little last night."

Duarte looked at Valkonen, giving him leave to ask a question.

"Arthritis?" he asked. "Your ankle, I mean."

Marta smiled. "Thank goodness, no. I turned my ankle skiing last January."

Duarte resumed her questioning. "Was Mr. MacShane letting you know he'd be out late?"

"Yes. He's very considerate."

"How late might he stay out?"

"These days, I'd expect him home by one or two a.m."

"It used to be later?"

"He used to stay out all night when he was younger and a print journalist."

"Did you ever accompany him?"

"Once or twice only. I grew up in Vienna. My life was ... more given to classical culture, shall we say. That and academia. And sports. Ian is a scholar in his own way, but I'm afraid we have different tastes in music."

Marta turned to look at Valkonen.

"You're very quiet, Sergeant. Are you the dispassionate onlooker? Watching for non-verbal suggestions? Perhaps wondering if Ian didn't go out with another woman last night?"

Valkonen shook his head. "The thought never entered my mind."

"But you are watching me closely."

"Observation is a part of my job," he admitted.

"Mine, too." With that she turned to Duarte. "I was wondering if you and the sergeant were intimate. I know that often happens when two people share a dangerous occupation."

Valkonen saw Duarte's face turn red. He couldn't tell if she was embarrassed or, more likely, getting mad.

Before Duarte could express her feelings, Marta said, "I've decided you're not. So, I think, the two of you are sharing some common concern. I don't feel as much worry coming from the sergeant as I do from you, Detective. So the difficulty you're facing doesn't include him personally."

The psychiatrist took a sip of her lemonade.

"We're not here to talk about me," Duarte said firmly.

Marta Waldman nodded. She pushed the file folder forward and tapped it twice.

"No, we're here to talk about this."

"And that would be?" Duarte asked.

"When my husband didn't appear for his broadcast this morning, I drove down to the radio station. I'm the only other person who has a key to his desk. The station manager was hoping I might find something that would explain Ian's absence. I found this."

Duarte looked at Valkonen again.

"Mr. MacShane made notes about our conversation with him yesterday?" he asked.

"Yes," Marta said.

"Did he mention he told us about his therapy with you?" Duarte asked.

"Yes."

"Now, you wish he'd talked a bit more to you last night, before he went out. Asked for your counsel."

"Exactly, Detective."

Marta nodded, as if she knew the policewoman felt the same way about whatever was worrying her. Tough as Duarte was, she still had to look away.

Valkonen took over.

"Since you know what we're facing, Doctor, what can you tell us about teens and suicide?"

She looked at Valkonen and he thought this woman's patients wouldn't spend years in therapy. She'd root out the cause of their problems in short order.

"Suicide is the third leading cause of death among American adolescents aged 10 to 19 years old," she said. "Only automobile accidents and homicide kill more of this age cohort. Approximately, 1 percent of teens attempt suicide and of those attempts 1 percent succeeds."

Valkonen did the math. "So we're talking one suicide death for every 10,000 kids."

"That's for the population at large. Which, contrary to popular imagery, enjoys relatively good mental health. When you look at groups suffering from major depression, bipolar disorder, conduct disorder, substance abuse, random psychological trauma such as a parental divorce, death of a family member or friend, loss of achieved or anticipated status, then 15-to-30 percent of affected teens go on to attempt suicide."

Duarte's face paled as she heard the numbers.

"Girls attempt suicide nine times more often than boys, but boys who attempt suicide are four times more likely to succeed. They are more apt to use guns."

As if Marta could sense Duarte's distress, she continued to look only at Valkonen.

"Are most suicides planned?" he asked.

"Most often, there's a pattern. Thinking about death. Wishing for death. Thinking about suicide. Making plans. Carrying out the attempt."

The words sounded textbook, but Valkonen could see in

Marta Waldman's eyes how they applied to her husband. She'd been through the drill with Ian MacShane, pulled him back from the brink, and now she was worrying that maybe she'd lost him after all.

She needed another drink of lemonade, and Duarte took one, too.

He said, "If that's the normal pattern, what else is there?"

"Impulsive suicide. No warning whatsoever. No chance for intervention."

The doctor's voice had softened; she was starting to withdraw into herself.

"What about group suicide?" Valkonen asked.

"Ah, yes." Marta's head bobbed sadly. "The companionship of leaving life serially or *en masse*. There's an undeniable if perverse attraction in that."

Valkonen thought about the extremes to which some people could play follow the leader and sighed. Then he noticed both of the women at the table with him had not only lapsed into silence but seemed to be physically compressing. Give them another minute or two and they'd disappear completely.

He intervened.

"Dr. Waldman, we're going to do everything we can to find Mr. MacShane. Alive and well. In the meantime, you said your grandson might be of help to us in finding the musical group we're looking for."

He'd spoken forcefully, hoping his tone would be taken for confidence, and it did seem to rouse both Marta and Duarte out of their self-absorption.

"Yes, of course, Sergeant," Marta said. "Let me give you Gregory's phone number — and then I think I'll lie down for a rest. My ankle is starting to hurt."

She gave him the number and Gregory surname, which the tape recorder duly noted, and said to tell Gregory that he'd be doing Grandmother a favor by helping them.

"If you'll excuse me now ..." she said.

Marta Waldman stood up and her stride, seemingly normal before, was now marked by a pronounced limp. Valkonen caught up with her and gave her support.

"Let me help you," he said.

She seemed grateful for it. Valkonen opened the rear door of the house for her. He saw Duarte coming up behind them, carrying the lemonade glasses and the file folder. They all went inside.

Valkonen said to Duarte, "Detective, why don't you help Doctor Waldman to her bed? I'll wait for you here." Then he had a thought, "Doctor, do you have a picture of Gregory so we'll know him when we see him?"

She told Valkonen to look for the framed picture of the handsome young man in the living room. He watched Duarte lead the older woman away. Then he went to find the picture of Gregory.

What he found was a picture of Waldo.

CHAPTER 12

As soon as Valkonen and Duarte left Marta Waldman's house, he told her that Ian MacShane's grandson was Waldo, but Duarte said she had to go home. "I keep my original duty weapon there, a .38 snubby."

"Yeah?"

"Didn't you hear what that woman said? Boys use guns."

"Don't you keep your weapons secured?"

"Of course, I do. I've got a small safe in my bedroom closet. But I'm thinking how Sebi got into my work computer to make his little peep show. Valkonen, my computer is password-protected. But Sebi got into it anyway. Who's to say he couldn't have come up with the combination to my safe somehow?"

Seemed possible — but so far there was no evidence the boy had ever come out of the ocean. Not that Valkonen was about to say that to Duarte.

"Okay, you go home," he said. "I'll bring Wal— I mean, I'll bring Gregory in for questioning."

"Where'll you do the interview?"

"Downtown. I wouldn't be surprised if Chief Barton gets in on it. Has words with the kid who invited his daughter to the death concert."

Duarte nodded. "Yeah, I would."

Then she said she had to go.

Using the telephone number Marta Waldman had given them and her grandson's full name, Gregory Meltzer, Valkonen accessed LAPD's reverse directory to find the boy's address. He was unpleasantly surprised to discover Gregory lived in Westwood only two blocks from Evie, Dana, and Jack.

The proximity of the three people he loved most to the kid who was recruiting for a mass-suicide show gave Valkonen a new sense of urgency. Helped him understand how Duarte was feeling. He drove more aggressively than usual on his way to the Meltzer house.

After he'd seen the picture of Gregory hanging on the wall of the MacShane-Waldman living room, Valkonen had gone back to the kitchen where Duarte had left the manila file folder she'd brought in from the yard, the one the doctor had taken from her husband's office. Opening the folder, he'd seen that the copy of Evie's sketch they'd left with Ian MacShane wasn't there. Dr. Waldman hadn't known her grandson was the boy they wanted.

But her husband had known.

He must've have gone to confront the boy — and now he

was missing.

Never one to think of himself as a hero, especially not now that he was so close to retirement, Valkonen called for backup to meet him at the Meltzer address.

He was promised two patrol units would respond to his call, but when he turned onto the block where Gregory Meltzer lived he found a far larger official presence: four black-and-whites, an LAFD truck, an ambulance, and an unmarked car, indicating detectives had been called.

He pulled to the curb, walked over to a uniformed officer maintaining the security perimeter, and identified himself.

The patrol cop was polite but underwhelmed, "You got some business here, Sarge?"

"The chief sent me," Valkonen replied. He gave the cop a phone number he could call to verify the claim. The patrolman wisely declined and allowed Valkonen to step inside the yellow tape and sign the log for personnel present at the crime scene.

"Who died?" Valkonen asked, thinking he'd hear MacShane's name.

But the cop said, "Some kid. They're having trouble deciding if it's homicide or suicide."

A kid? Maybe a suicide? Oh, shit.

Valkonen's stomach turned over.

The two dicks running the scene were from the West L.A. Division, a matched pair — tall, lean, slicked-back hair — so closely resembling one another they could have been taken for brothers, but they identified themselves as Shanley and DiLeo.

Unlike the uniformed cop, they took Valkonen up on his offer to call the chief's number. Detectives were a skeptical lot. But doubt turned to dutiful subordination when the chief himself answered DiLeo's call.

Valkonen could hear the chief's voice clearly over DiLeo's cell phone, and he had to repress a smile as DiLeo's posture straightened as he got an earful of direct orders.

"Yes, sir ... yes, sir ... I understand sir," DiLeo said.

Clicking off, he cast a baleful look at Valkonen.

"You've got our complete cooperation, Sergeant Valkonen. Per the chief's orders."

Each detective looked like he'd swallowed a rat. No cop liked to have his place in the pecking order disturbed. It screwed with his self-image, insulted his manhood.

Valkonen understood that and sought to make peace. Guys worked better together when nobody had a hard-on.

"You detectives mind if I bring you up to date on why my partner and I have been looking for this kid?" A thought occurred to Valkonen: he'd better make sure there was no misunderstanding here. "We are talking about Gregory Meltzer, right?"

"Yeah, him," Shanley said, not yet ready to thaw.

"Okay, well let me tell you what I have then."

Despite themselves, the two dicks leaned forward.

Nobody enjoyed a cop story more than another cop.

"So what do you think, Sarge?" DiLeo asked.

Valkonen and the two detectives had entered the Meltzer house after Valkonen had told them the story of the suicide concert and how Gregory had passed along the story to the chief's daughter. That information legitimized Valkonen's presence to the two dicks, but in their eyes the right thing for Valkonen to do now would be to pass the whole thing along to them. They were better qualified to pursue it.

They also weren't at the ends of their careers like Valkonen was.

Cracking this sucker would make them legends.

Trying hard to be subtle in light of Valkonen working directly for the chief, they were now soliciting his opinion whether Gregory Meltzer had taken his own life or had died at the hands of another. The boy's body lay at their feet in the living room of the house.

Gregory was face up, his eyes open. It was amazing how well Evie had captured his likeness, sight unseen. He hadn't been dead long enough for any bugs to get to him. He looked as if he might simply be stoned, staring at the ceiling, listening to music only he could hear. There was no exsanguination. No bruising to any visible area of skin. No needle marks. No visible reason at all why a boy in his late teens should have died.

But there was a bullet hole in the wall. Sizable one. Splashed plaster dust on the carpet ... along with some particulate heavier than the plaster. Something reflective.

Glass?

Then Valkonen had it.

He asked the detectives, "You gentlemen take the framed photo off the wall? The one the heavy-caliber slug passed through. Or did the shot knock it down?"

Shanley and DiLeo exchanged a look.

"The shot," Shanley said. "Crime scene team photographed it *in situ* and took it away."

"But you got a look at the subject of the photo before

it went."

"Kid's parents. Studio portrait," DiLeo responded.

"And where are they?"

"According to a calendar hanging in the kitchen, Italy," Shanley said. "Due home this coming Saturday."

Valkonen closed his eyes momentarily. Thought of Jack. Prayed he'd never hear of his son dying while he was away somewhere.

DiLeo prompted Valkonen. "So you got an opinion, Sarge? How the kid died."

"Who spotted the body?" Valkonen asked.

"Mailman," Shanley said.

"No sign anyone broke into the house?"

"No."

"You find the gun that fired the shot?" Valkonen asked.

The two dicks shook their heads.

"You have the time yet to talk to any of the neighbors? See how the family got along?"

"On our to-do list," Shanley replied.

Valkonen looked around. Other than the dead body and the hole in the wall, the room was a fine example of genteel Southland living. Everything in its place.

"The rest of the house this well kept?" he asked.

"Except the kid's room," DiLeo said. "It's a pigsty."

"Any sign of drugs in the pigsty?" Valkonen asked.

Shanley shrugged. "Some of the mold growing on the windowsill might be hallucinogenic. Other than that, we didn't find anything on the first pass."

The sum of the detective's answers told Valkonen that the Meltzers, parents and child, respected one another's boundaries. Maybe even held affection for each other. It happened, even in L.A. Even when there was a daddy with only one mommy.

"Somebody killed Gregory," Valkonen said. "Or caused him to kill himself."

"No sign of a struggle," DiLeo said, looking down at the body.

"And how do you persuade a teenage kid to off himself?" Shanley wanted to know.

Valkonen looked at them.

"You put a bullet through a picture of Mom and Dad. Tell the kid they get it if he doesn't do himself. And/or you show him what a high-powered slug can do to a wall and say he's going to die a messy death if he doesn't choose a clean, neat, maybe painless one."

DiLeo offered a rebuttal. "Or junior here didn't get along with the old man and old lady. He plugs their picture before he does himself."

"You'd have found the gun, if that's what happened," Valkonen told him. "No way Gregory shoots the picture one day, and gets rid of the gun, and kills himself the next day."

"You'd be amazed the strange stuff a detective sees, Sarge," Shanley said.

"I'm sure I would. I'd even make a small allowance for that possibility if you hadn't told me about Mr. and Mrs. Metzger coming home this weekend."

"What's that got to do with it?" DiLeo asked.

"Either of you two have kids?" Valkonen wanted to know.

The two dicks shook their heads.

"Well, don't believe everything you see on TV about Mom and Dad being totally clueless all the time. More often, they can see when something's seriously wrong."

Evie and Dana always knew when something was bothering Jack. And one way or another Duarte had found out about Sebastian's escapade down in Mexico with poor dead Audra Stevens.

"My opinion," Valkonen told the detectives, "somebody knew that Gregory knew the details about the death concert, knew when his parents were coming back, and were afraid he'd let the cat out of the bag. Mom and Dad would call the cops and ruin the whole thing."

Shanley and DiLeo shared another silent exchange.

Then Shanley conceded, "What you told us, maybe we can see that, too."

"Yeah, but you got any idea who our perp is?" DiLeo asked.

Valkonen gave them his best guess. Hoping like hell he was wrong.

Valkonen was back in the Z, sitting there wondering if he should have opened his mouth to the two dicks. Could Ian MacShane really have killed his grandson? He'd certainly known Gregory was the boy Valkonen and Duarte had wanted to find. The sketch Evie had done of Gregory was bang on. MacShane could have directed them to his grandson immediately, but he hadn't.

Why not?

Who could say? Maybe MacShane was simply protecting someone dear to him. But, really, there was no telling how he felt about the boy. MacShane and his grandson could have been estranged for all Valkonen knew.

Maybe MacShane was sick. Terminal even. He was old enough for something like that. If that was the case and the end was inevitable, a man who'd already considered suicide might want to go out in a way that would make him a featured name in what would become a rock 'n' roll legend.

Be a pretty cruel thing to do to Marta Waldman, though, after she'd saved his ass once before, and was worried sick about him now. But who knew how MacShane felt about her? Hell, even if he did love her, he could still be a selfish enough prick to want to end his life his own way.

Which he wouldn't have been able to do if he'd given up Gregory. Whatever the case, Valkonen never would have pegged MacShane as a killer. Especially, not someone who'd kill his own grandson.

Now, it was up to Shanley and DiLeo to see if they could find any evidence to implicate MacShane in Gregory's death, and they were welcome to that job. Valkonen had promised the detectives they could have all the credit on the LAPD end of the case, but he'd extracted a promise that they would keep him informed of any developments on their end.

And he'd left it to the two dicks to tell Gregory Meltzer's parents their son was dead.

CHAPTER 13

Joan Duarte took the precaution of calling Valkonen's cell number before fighting traffic all the way to downtown L.A.

The way she put it, "These days, any time I drive east of La Brea, I feel like I'm halfway to Kansas."

Valkonen started to ask, "Never ... nah, forget it."

"What?"

"I almost fell into a little ethnic insensitivity."

"The hell you talkin' about?"

Valkonen cleared his throat. "I was about to ask if your family ever lived in East L.A."

"Prick."

"See. I told you I shouldn't have said anything."

"Next time I'll listen," Duarte said. "This time, I'll tell you no. We never lived in East L.A. My dad wouldn't have it. Said we're Americans; we weren't going to live in any barrio.

I grew up in Culver City."

"You speak Spanish, though, right?"

"Only because I took four years of it in high school."

"How about your son?"

"Where you going with all this, Valkonen?"

"I was just thinking, before you called, where Sebastian might be." Assuming he hadn't drowned, Valkonen thought but didn't say.

"Sebi doesn't speak any Spanish. Maybe a few curse words he hears from me, on the rare occasion I lose my temper. He's taking Latin."

Valkonen didn't think they'd find Sebastian hiding among any group of classical scholars, but from what his new partner had told him the boy was unlikely to be hiding in any immigrant enclave either. Which eliminated vast sections of the city.

Again, assuming that he was still alive.

As if she could read his mind, Duarte said, "My .38 was in the safe."

Which was a mixed blessing.

"You never told me, Joan," Valkonen said, "is Sebi a good swimmer?"

"Yeah, he is. He ..." Her voice broke but the lapse of control was only momentary. "He was on this swim team at the park near our house. He won trophies in the 50 and 100-meter races. Back when he was in middle school, you know."

Her voice trailed off at the end as if she was eulogizing her son. Valkonen said, "That's good. He spent a lot time in the water, he wouldn't panic."

"No, he wouldn't. I've thought about that. What might've made the difference, though, was not being able to save Audra. She must've got away from him somehow. Who knows how much time he spent looking for her? He could've gotten tired. Too tired to ..."

Valkonen was still sitting in his car outside the Meltzer house. He knew he and Duarte should be having this conversation in person not over the phone.

"Joan, you hate coincidences the way any good cop does?"

"Of course." Her voice was so quiet he almost didn't hear her.

"I didn't know about Sebi being a champion swimmer before. If I had, I would have said there's no way anyone but your son posed Audra's body the way it was found. It's too much like that picture of him and her on that beach in Mexico."

Even as he said those words, Valkonen found them personally convincing. What had started out as a way to prop up Duarte became a persuasive argument. Her son was likely alive. Likely, not certainly, because you could hate coincidences all you wanted but they still existed.

Most often, they existed when they could knock you on your ass.

Still, Duarte agreed with him. Her voice firmed up.

"Yeah," she said. "You're right, damnit. That had to be Sebi who did that."

"You're at home, right?" Valkonen asked.

"Yeah."

"Meet me at the Third Street Promenade at Santa Monica Boulevard in twenty minutes."

"What about your interrogation of Waldo? I mean Gregory. You done with that? You get anything from him?"

Valkonen told her about Gregory Meltzer's death.

"Jesus Christ. He was our only lead."

"There's still Ian MacShane, if he's still alive. And if he

wants to go to the death concert, it's a good bet he is."

The silence at Duarte's end of the line was long enough for him to think he might have lost the call signal. "Joan? You there?"

"Yeah, I was just thinking. You know, trying to find Gregory Meltzer was so hard because he was just a nameless kid. But people all over town know Ian MacShane, especially people in the music business. It should be easier to find him."

Valkonen liked that thought.

"Yeah, I'll get right on that. Forget about meeting me."

"Hey, what'm I going to do?"

"You're going to talk to every friend of Sebi's you can find, his teachers, too. Maybe one of them has misplaced sympathies and took him in. He had to go somewhere when he came out of the ocean."

Valkonen heard what he imagined to be the sound of Duarte slapping her forehead.

"Jesus, how could I be so stupid?" she asked.

"You were in shock, Joan. Probably still are."

"Damn dumb is what I am."

Valkonen didn't want to do it but he had to lead her one step farther.

"Joan, if Sebi wasn't interested in going to the death concert before Audra died, he might be now. Assuming he's heard about it. And we both know how that goes."

"Yeah," she said, "kids usually find trouble before we can find them."

CHAPTER 14

Valkonen put a different spin on Ian MacShane's disappearance when he went to see Aeneas Terry, the station manager at KDSW. He suggested the possibility that MacShane may have been kidnapped.

Terry was African-American, an inch or two shorter than Valkonen with the wiry build of a Kenyan marathoner. His hair was closely cut and going gray at the temples. He wore a tweed sport coat over a white oxford-cloth shirt and blue jeans. On his feet was a pair of Chuck Taylor low-cut olive green monochromes. Terry looked at the world through gold wire-frame glasses.

On the wall behind his desk, in a silver frame, was a photo from the New York Times: Terry and Ed Koch wearing tuxes with Barbra Streisand standing between them. Next to that were Terry's two diplomas from Columbia:

B.A. in Anthropology; M.A. in Journalism.

The look the station manager was giving Valkonen told him that Terry wasn't just book-smart; he'd learned a lesson or two on the streets of New York as well.

Wouldn't be an easy guy to scam.

It helped that Valkonen felt what he told Terry was plausible.

Maybe even true. MacShane might have been kidnapped.

"So you've contacted the FBI, kidnapping being a federal crime," Terry said.

Valkonen thought Terry could work on-air with the voice he had.

"No, sir. I don't have the evidence yet for that."

"Then you've come to enlist my aid to develop the evidence?"

"I'm trying to find Mr. MacShane myself. As fast as I can."

"Even if Ian's unexplained absence is strictly a local police matter, you're still out of your bailiwick, Sergeant."

"I'm working with Detective Joan Duarte of the SMPD on a larger case, which now involves Mr. MacShane and crosses jurisdictions."

"Nicely said, Sergeant. Where did you go to school?"

Valkonen blinked at the question. "College? Loyola Marymount."

"Where you studied?"

"Philosophy ... with a minor in screenwriting."

Terry bought it for maybe two seconds.

With a smile he said, "The screenwriting joke was pretty good. A cop studying philosophy, though, that might take a little while to figure out."

"Not really," Valkonen said. "Making inquiries into

human nature is vocational training for cops."

"I suppose so, you put it like that. Now why don't you really tell me what's happening with Ian?"

As with most cops, Valkonen didn't like to share with civilians. The reasons were both tribal and practical. But Valkonen could see he was in *quid pro quo* territory. So he told Terry about the death concert, the meeting he and Duarte had with MacShane, how MacShane had held back the identity of his grandson, Gregory Meltzer, the discussion with Marta Waldman, and Gregory's death. All of which he asked the station manager to hold in confidence.

Terry absorbed Valkonen's words stoically and then nodded.

Then he conceded, "Ian might have been kidnapped."

Having gone that far, Valkonen decided to offer his opinion of the situation. Terry would likely reach the same conclusions on his own.

"That or he's dead. That or—"

"He had a hand in his grandson's death," Terry voiced the possibility but he shook his head at the same time.

"You don't think so," Valkonen said.

"I *hope* he didn't, but you never know about people, do you?"

"Different philosophers offer differing opinions," Valkonen told him.

Aeneas Terry let Valkonen into Ian MacShane's office. Marta Waldman had left MacShane's desk unlocked after she'd found the file holding her husband's notes on his talk with Valkonen and Duarte. The station manager called Doctor Waldman to obtain her permission to allow a further search of MacShane's papers, but Marta wasn't answering her phone.

Valkonen winced. He'd forgotten that Shanley and DiLeo, if they'd been unable to reach Gregory's parents in Italy, would have looked for, and probably found, the closest local family member to notify. Marta. Who was already reeling from her husband's disappearance.

He shared his concern with Terry, who volunteered to drive over to the MacShane-Waldman house and see if Marta was all right. Keep her company.

This time Valkonen felt bad about burdening someone else with the grieving relative, but he put that aside and started his search of Ian MacShane's business calendar and Rolodex.

CHAPTER 15

Joan Duarte was on the walkway outside the cafeteria at Santa Monica High School, SAMOHI to everyone in the school community, on her way to the administrative offices when she remembered that her son was missing a day of school and she hadn't called in to excuse his absence. She could hardly blame herself for that, but thinking about it now, she had to wonder why the school hadn't called her home to ask why Sebi wasn't in attendance.

She'd checked her message machine when she'd gotten home and there was no call from SAMOHI. Definitely something to discuss with Principal Helen Liszt, who'd agreed to see the detective on short notice.

Valkonen's Policework 101 suggestion — check with the missing kid's friends — had led her to the school, which was where Sebi's friends should be right now. In classes. Or eating lunch in the cafeteria. Duarte glanced at the groups of kids she passed. All of them felt the weight of her regard, and they all fell silent as they looked back at her.

Keeping her apart from their conversations, holding back their secrets, that was normal teenage behavior around any adult. But she also got the feeling that these kids, unlike most people on the street, had made her as a cop.

Duarte could imagine what would happen if she asked Helen Liszt to call an assembly of the student body. Without a doubt, there would be kids in the audience who could give her chapter and verse on the death concert, where it would be held, the date and time. Tell her the name of the band. But would they reveal themselves, the ones who knew? Would they open up to her? Maybe if she got the chance to go at them hard in an interrogation room. But that wasn't going to happen because no one with any knowledge would ever step forward. The things teenagers kept to themselves these days were truly insane.

How many school shootings had happened because the kids who knew what was coming hadn't warned their parents or a teacher? Pretty much all of them.

Duarte was about to reach for the door to the admin building when it opened from the inside. A boy Duarte took to be a senior saw her, smiled, and politely held the door for her. Great looking kid, but there were lots of great looking kids at the school. SAMOHI had produced any number of Hollywood actors — and one Watergate felon, John Ehrlichmann.

Duarte met the polite young man's eyes. "Thanks."

"You're welcome, ma'am."

Ma'am. Made Duarte feel maternal. So she went with that.

"Everything going okay?"

"Couldn't be better." His smile got brighter. He looked around to see if anyone was watching. Then he shared a confidence. "I just heard from my agent."

"Yeah?"

The boy nodded, clearly on Cloud Nine. "Had to get an excused absence from school next week. Can't say more."

Duarte asked a question anyway. "Lot of guys at the audition?"

"Line went down the block." He gave her a wave goodbye.

Duarte went inside, her perspective clarified.

The kid she'd just talked to, the one who got the part, he had everything to live for; the other ones in the block-long line, they might be interested in taking in a concert soon. Young people just didn't know a strong-willed human being could bounce back from most anything.

Duarte identified herself to the principal's secretary.

She sure hoped Helen Liszt could identify Sebi's friends for her.

Because other than poor, dead Audra, she didn't have a clue who they were.

CHAPTER 16

Ian MacShane's calendar had morphed from the schedule of a busy professional to a list of missed appointments and irate colleagues — at least until the people on the other end of Valkonen's phone calls learned that a policeman was on the line and asking for help in determining MacShane's whereabouts. No one was able to help him. Without exception, though, they expressed concern for the radio personality's well-being and promised to call Valkonen if they heard from him. Being held in such universally high regard impressed Valkonen; usually public figures attracted at least a few snarky detractors.

Not MacShane. Even when Valkonen discreetly inquired if the Englishman might have slipped away to a rehab facility without letting anyone know, he was assured by everyone he talked to that Ian MacShane was clean and sober, had been for decades. He had banished the demons of drink, drugs, and sex long ago. His life was his love of music and his wife.

Which made Valkonen think to request that each of the people he talked to not bother Marta Waldman for the time being. She was distraught enough without receiving a raft of calls from friends whose anxiety he'd roused.

Valkonen moved on to MacShane's Rolodex and started riffling through it. He was immediately whisked away on a magical mystery tour. MacShane had Sir Paul's home phone number. There were also cards for Mick and Keith. Eric, Pete, and Roger, too. Valkonen had never thought of himself as starstruck, but his head reeled as he flipped through the names. Everyone who was anyone in rock music, the kind he liked, was present in MacShane's Rolodex. Bruce was there. The roll call filled his head to bursting with music.

None of it doing him a damn bit of good.

But there were other names, too. Promoters, on-air colleagues at radio stations around the country, lawyers ... a priest? Valkonen copied the priest's name and number. A yellow reminder note was stuck on the card for Michael Telephus — Mickey T., the manager at Clive's. Or possibly the reminder was intended for Walter Thornberry. The doorman's name also appeared on Mickey T.'s card, along with a separate phone number. The message on the note was only two words: *Call tomorrow.*

If the message had been written yesterday, the call was meant to be placed today.

To one of the two men at Clive's. Valkonen would call them both.

Another yellow note flagged the name of a doctor. Not a shrink but an internist at the UCLA Med Center. As with the other reminder, this one also said: *Call tomorrow.*

Reading the second note gave Valkonen a sinking feeling. Had he been right in speculating that MacShane might be ill? Maybe he had been keeping the news from his wife, determined to die at a place and time of his own choosing.

But if that was the case, the question remained: Why would a dying man kill his own grandson? Valkonen just couldn't see it. Not unless some extreme provocation had set MacShane off. Most people hoped their families would continue in perpetuity. Valkonen certainly wanted Jack to live on long after he was gone, and the thought of having a grandson someday, it was almost too much to hope for. He'd met MacShane only the one time but it was long enough to get a decent read on him. He didn't see him as a killer.

Of course, he might have to revise that impression after he talked to MacShane's doctor.

First, though, he'd make the calls to Clive's, start with Walter.

Valkonen was seated behind MacShane's desk, but he used his own phone. He didn't know where his investigation might lead but to be safe he didn't want to leave any record of it on someone else's phone line.

Clive's wouldn't open for hours, but Walter Thornberry picked up on the first ring, announcing the club's name.

"Hey, Walter. It's Sergeant Valkonen."

"Great minds," Walter replied.

"Pardon?"

"Great minds, they think alike. I was just about to call you."

"Yeah? What's up?"

"You want me to go first?"

"Sure."

"That kid you're looking for, I remember where I saw him."

Might not matter any more now that Gregory Meltzer had been found dead, but Valkonen had learned never to cut anyone off.

Walter said, "The kid was with this other dude, name of Jimmy Bern, B-E-R-N. Reason I didn't remember before now is Jimmy didn't introduce the kid to me. Still don't know his name. But Jimmy can tell you."

"What's Jimmy do?" Valkonen asked.

"Scuffle mostly. He's trying to set himself up in the music management biz. One of his groups, maybe his only group far as I know, he was trying to get them a gig here."

A bell rang in Valkonen's head. Music management? That was the direction the Beverly Hills cop, Drury, had pointed him. Drury had said even the greenest band had some kind of manager. And now Walter was telling him Gregory Meltzer had been seen in the company of a wannabe music mogul.

"You have a phone and address for Jimmy Bern?" Valkonen asked.

"Of course. Jimmy had his way he'd've tattooed 'em on my arm." Walter gave Valkonen the information. "Think that'll help you find the kid you want?"

"I think it's going to be a big help."

"So what'd you want to talk to me about?"

Valkonen asked Walter if he'd heard from or was expecting a call from Ian MacShane.

"Unh-uh. I know him. Told him about my plans to have my own place. But mostly he deals with Mickey T. when he comes here."

"Mickey in?" Valkonen asked.

"Sorry. He called in sick. Left me in charge the rest of the week."

Valkonen didn't like hearing the club manager, like Ian MacShane, was suddenly absent from his normal post.

"You think you could give me Mickey's home phone number?"

Walter was silent for a long moment.

Then he said, "Never hurts to be on the good side of the police, does it?"

"Never does," Valkonen agreed.

Walter gave him the number.

CHAPTER 17

Helen Liszt, the principal of SAMOHI, listened to Joan Duarte's tale of Audra Stevens' drowning and Sebastian Duarte's disappearance. The principal's eyes showed concern but otherwise her demeanor remained stoic. That changed when Duarte asked her why the school hadn't called her home asking for an explanation of Sebi's absence.

Losing a student to a tragic accident or an act of self-destruction was a sorrow any big-city principal had to accept, but learning there was a breakdown in something as fundamental as tracking unexcused absences was a problem to be addressed immediately.

Liszt picked up her phone and buzzed her secretary. "Candace, Sebastian Duarte, sophomore class, isn't in school today. His mother didn't call to report his absence and we didn't call the Duarte home to ask for an explanation. Please call Millie Henderson and find out why not." She also asked the secretary to talk personally to all of Sebastian's teachers and ask them with whom Sebastian socialized. Putting the phone down, she looked at Duarte.

"Do you think ..." Helen Liszt began.

She paused to think of the best way to word her question.

Duarte knew where she was going. "That Sebi could have drowned, too? Sure. That was the first thing I thought." Just saying as much started to chill Duarte so she pushed on. "But now I think he's alive ... and afraid to come home."

Liszt nodded. What kid wouldn't be afraid to face his parents, especially a mother who was a cop, after being involved in an episode where a friend died?

The principal's phone buzzed. "Yes, Candace? I see. No, please ask Millie to come to my office and bring the print-out."

Duarte had no problem reading the principal's face. The problem Duarte had brought to her had just gotten worse somehow.

"What is it?" Duarte asked.

The principal leaned forward, resting her elbows on her desk. "Joan, the times we've met, you've always struck me as a woman with both feet on the ground."

"Yeah?" Duarte said guardedly.

"And I imagine your job calls for composure in trying moments."

"It does and I'm pretty good at it."

Except for punching out the occasional creep who groped her. Or now, getting impatient with Helen Liszt.

"With that in mind," the principal said, "is it possible you called the school this morning and forgot about it?"

Duarte was stunned. "What? No, no way. I didn't call."

Liszt sighed. "Please forgive me for asking, but we have a record of *someone* calling from your home phone number, saying Sebastian wouldn't be in school today due to illness."

For just a moment, Duarte's mouth fell open. Then she closed it and started thinking. Her condo was wired to prevent burglaries. Sebi knew the password to disable the alarm, of course. But she had looked hard when she'd gone home and had seen absolutely no sign that her son or anyone else had been there in her absence. So how could ...

A cop thought came to her — Valkonen would be proud — and she felt sure it was right.

"Helen," she asked, "you know what a phone phreak is?"

The principal nodded. "A computer hacker who games the phone system."

"Right. You got any students here might fit the bill?"

"Do you really think—"

"What I think, someone routed a call through my phone, and someone else, say a girl with acting ability, pretended to be me calling in."

The principal closed her eyes momentarily, absorbing the blow.

When she opened her eyes, Duarte hit her with another punch.

"Somebody did this for Sebi, you need to find out how widespread the con is."

There was a knock at the door. Helen Liszt looked as if she welcomed the distraction as she told the visitor to enter. A young woman wearing glasses and an expectant look on her face stepped into the principal's office. She held a piece of paper in her hand.

Liszt introduced her, "Millie Henderson, Detective Joan Duarte. The detective has told me she didn't make the call to school this morning."

Henderson looked at Duarte, baffled. She held up the paper in her hand.

"But ..."

"Millie, is Candace at her desk?"

"No.

"Will you please go get Mr. Breit and Doctor Spaneas for me? Right away."

The young woman nodded. She put the sheet of paper she'd brought with her on the principal's desk, a statement that she'd done her job, and then she left.

"I've just summoned the heads of the math and science faculties," Helen Liszt told Duarte. "They'll know if any of our students could manage the technical end of this deception. We'll start there, and we'll get to the bottom of this right away."

The principal started tapping a pencil on her desk.

Looking pissed but in control.

Duarte thought she might make a pretty good cop.

Tony Breit and George Spaneas both came up with the same name: Fabio Stanley.

"Kid's only a sophomore," Breit told Duarte, "but without a doubt he's the most gifted mathematical thinker on campus. Including the faculty. Including me."

Spaneas nodded and said, "Same in science. Chemistry, physics, you name it. The kid gobbles up text books the way other kids read comic books."

Duarte looked at Helen Liszt.

"A kid like that, you had to suspect him."

The principal bobbed her head. "I did. I just wanted you

to hear my suspicion validated by others."

"What's going on here?" the science teacher asked.

Liszt told them about the phone phreaking.

"I know for a fact Fabio's built his own laptop," Spaneas said.

"Wrote the OS for it, too," Breit said.

"Regular little Einstein, huh?" Duarte asked.

"Fabio could be in college right now," Helen Liszt told her, "doing post-grad work."

"So why isn't ..." Duarte stopped, figured out the answer. "He's here because he likes it here. He's made a niche for himself. And maybe going off to college with older students is intimidating. Is Fabio small, physically?"

Liszt told her, "He's not short, but he is slight. And, yes, he's well regarded by most of the student body."

"Prized is more like it," Breit said.

"Fabio does some amazing scouting reports for all the sports teams," Spaneas added. "He's made being a geek cool."

Duarte nodded and looked at Helen Liszt. "This phony absence con, I bet every kid here knows about it." She sighed and gazed at all three educators. "My Sebi's not in this boy's league but he's pretty smart. He and Fabio know each other? Hang together?"

The principal said they did.

"Sebastian is one of the few kids Fabio can talk to substantively," Spaneas told her.

Breit agreed. "It takes a little coaxing sometimes, but Sebi can often make intuitive leaps. Understand what Fabio's telling him. The two of them, sometimes they're like kids playing with new toys."

Helen Liszt said, "Most of us hope that Fabio will

become one of his generation's greatest teachers. Now ... now, I think we'd better call him in."

Duarte held up a hand. "Wait. This boy have a custodial mom or dad?"

"His parents are still married," Liszt told her.

Which was enough to surprise Duarte. Southern California boy genius and phone phreak, she'd figured there had to be something dysfunctional in his background.

"How about that? Before we get to Fabio, let's call the parents in, assuming they can get away from work — and please don't tell me one or both of them are lawyers."

"No," the principal told her. "Mrs. Stanley is an artist, a watercolorist. Mr. Stanley is retired."

"From what?" Duarte wanted to know.

Helen Liszt said, "He was a rather successful rock musician."

CHAPTER 18

Valkonen drove from KDSW to the Westwood location of the UCLA Medical Center to see Rupert Ralph, M.D., the internist listed on Ian MacShane's call reminder. The doc's name made Valkonen think he was English, a Brit expat like MacShane. Given the professional ethic that a physician didn't reveal a patient's medical history, and the likelihood that the doc shared ethnic ties with MacShane, Valkonen had thought a phone call would be pointless. He'd get a brushoff; if he pushed, a disconnection.

Far better to show up unannounced. Flash the badge. Declare a life-and-death situation. Undoubtedly, Doctor Ralph would still withhold MacShane's history. But as Marta Waldman had commented, Valkonen was a close observer of people's behavior.

He would see how Rupert Ralph reacted when he

informed the doctor that he knew about MacShane's past brush with suicide. That and the fact that the radio personality had disappeared. If necessary, he'd add mention of Gregory Meltzer's death.

Hit the man with a flurry of emotional punches. See if that lessened his sense of ethical restraint. If not, Valkonen was sure he'd be able to see if the physician knew something the investigating officer didn't. Guilty knowledge was something any good cop could spot, and Valkonen was better at it than most. It was a plan, anyway.

The shame was, he didn't get the chance to use it.

The receptionist, a young blonde looking up from her copy of *Sports Illustrated*, told him, "Sorry, Doctor Ralph isn't in. He's canceled all his appointments for the week."

Valkonen frowned. "How come?"

The receptionist bit her lip, uncomfortable with the question.

"He went to some professional conference?" Valkonen suggested.

She almost went with that, but he could see she didn't want to lie to a cop.

"No," she replied.

"Well, if it's anything embarrassing, I don't need the details."

"Oh, no, it's nothing like that. But it is personal."

"Okay. We've got personal but not embarrassing. We're making progress. What else can you tell me?"

"He had to leave the country. Go back to the UK. Not because he had to. Well, I guess he did have to, but it's ... a family thing. Can we leave it at that?"

"Sure," Valkonen said. He'd pushed only a little; they were still friends. She smiled at him, happy he hadn't been a hardass with her.

"I'd still like to ask one or two more questions," he said.

She frowned. "I'm really not supposed to talk about what goes on around here, you know. There are rules and the doctors can get really touchy about them."

Valkonen nodded, the picture of understanding. Didn't raise a word of objection.

Didn't go away either.

The young blonde asked, "They're not about medical histories, your questions, are they? Because I definitely can't talk about that."

Valkonen shook his head.

"Will I get in trouble if I don't talk to you?"

"Probably not." His words were telling her she was off the hook, but she was smart enough to realize they weren't done.

"What's the catch then?" she asked.

"You ever beat yourself up for not doing something that could have saved somebody a lot of trouble? A *lot* of trouble."

The question found its mark, had more effect than Valkonen anticipated.

"Yes," she said quietly.

"It's like that. You'll feel terrible if you don't help me. For a long time."

It took her maybe five seconds to make up her mind.

Then she let Valkonen ask his question and checked her records to find the answers.

Yes, Doctor Ralph had taken a phone call from Mr. MacShane yesterday. And, yes, Doctor Ralph's family situation had come up almost immediately after that. What a coincidence.

Just like Mickey T. getting sick and taking off the rest of

the week.

Valkonen thanked the young receptionist for her help. Assured her she'd done the right thing. Left his business card with her and said he'd be happy to help her if she ever needed it.

Then he went back to his car and called Chief Barton.

The chief got in touch with the feds and ten minutes later Valkonen learned that Dr. Rupert Ralph had not flown out of L.A. to London or anywhere else in the past 24 hours. Nor was he booked on any airline to leave the country in the next 24 hours.

Thirty minutes after that, Valkonen found that Mickey T. wasn't answering his phone and didn't come to the door of his Marina Del Rey condo when Valkonen rang his doorbell, repeatedly. He barely resisted the temptation to kick in the club manager's door. Succeeding, in part, because he remembered Duarte telling him she'd hurt herself kicking a door.

"Thank you, Joan," he muttered to himself.

Then he went to see the priest whose name he'd found in MacShane's Rolodex.

Reverend Alan Purdy, pastor of St. Andrew By the Sea Episcopal Church in Santa Monica, unlike everyone else Valkonen was looking for, hadn't disappeared. He was in his place of worship talking to an electrician about a lighting problem the church was having. Without any attempt at eavesdropping, Valkonen could overhear their every word in the large, all but empty space. He waited at the back of the church until the two men finished their discussion.

Father Purdy, who'd spotted Valkonen the moment he'd

entered the church, came over to him and asked if he might be of help.

Valkonen identified himself. "Your secretary said I'd find you here. Is there somewhere we might talk for a few minutes?"

"Of course," the priest said.

He led Valkonen to a garden at one side of the church. Lush plantings shielded the men from the street. Purdy gestured to Valkonen to sit on a semi-circular stone bench. The priest sat opposite him.

"Now, what can I do for you, Sergeant?" he asked.

Valkonen came straight to the point. "Ian MacShane has disappeared. I'm looking for him. I found a card in Mr. MacShane's Rolodex with your name and number. I thought I'd ask if you'd heard from him recently."

"You've talked to Marta?"

"She called me. I went to her house. She's very worried."

Purdy looked more than a little concerned himself.

"So, she doesn't know where Ian is?"

"No."

A moment passed in silence. Shafts of sunlight found crevices in the canopy of leaves, the rays striking the priest, leaving Valkonen in shadow.

"I saw Ian in church last night," Purdy said.

Not long after he and Duarte had told MacShane about the death concert.

"Was there a service, Father?"

"No. The church is open in the early evening so people might pray after their day's labor. Ian was in a pew. He'd just lit a votive candle. I had no intention of disturbing him, but he came to me. Asked if I might remember him in my prayers."

Valkonen hated to ask, but he did. "Any particular reason?"

"I wouldn't be free to tell you if he'd given me a specific reason, but all he said was he could use the help of someone closer to God than he was."

A breeze stirred the leaves, letting the sun shine on Valkonen, revealing his disappointment to the priest.

"He did say one other thing," Purdy said. "He asked if he might call me soon, at a moment's notice, to be of help to the community. I said of course."

Valkonen looked at the priest with renewed interest.

"If Ian gets in touch with me, shall I tell him he needs to call you?" the priest asked.

Valkonen gave the priest one of his business cards.

"If you hold any moral sway over Mr. MacShane, insist on it, Father."

Jimmy Bern, the wannabe music mogul that Walter Thornberry had seen with Gregory Meltzer, was also among the missing. His office in a nondescript building on the Pico fringe of Beverly Hills was locked and dark. There wasn't even a receptionist to question.

Another door Valkonen would have liked to kick open.

But he only said, "Shit." And left.

He'd just entered the Z when his cell phone rang. Caller ID said it was Evie.

"Hi, Sis," he said, trying not to sound dispirited.

"Rick, we might have found something for you. Well, Dana did really."

Evie was clearly excited, but Valkonen didn't want to get his hopes up.

"What?" he asked.

"You remember I said Dana would ask her nieces and nephews if they'd heard of a great new band, one that would have escaped the notice of all us old farts?"

"Yeah?" Despite his earlier resolve, Valkonen felt his mood start to lift.

"They came up with one. But only after Dana coaxed it out of them. They were kind of embarrassed to let her know what it was. But they unanimously agreed it was really hot. Dana got them to burn a copy for us. Let us have the jewel box it came in, too. The cover art is primitive but, Rick, we listened to the music. It's very disturbing but also very good. Really rocks. Probably sell a *lot* of copies if they went commercial with it."

Valkonen's optimism rose even higher, so much so that he consciously had to rein it in. "Could be just a coincidence. All the bands out there, a few of them have to be good."

Evie said, "Rick, we're sure this is the group you want. Ask me its name."

"What's the name?"

"Death Penalty."

"Jesus," Valkonen said. Evie had to be right. "Does the CD cover list any names of the guys in the band? Please tell me there's an address on it, even a P.O. box."

Evie said, "Sorry. No address. No band members identified. But there is one name."

"Who?"

"Their manager. Somebody named Jimmy Bern. B-E-R-N."

CHAPTER 19

Jeff Stanley showed Duarte a tattoo on his right shoulder and bicep: a crucifix above text rendered in a gothic typeface, "Goin' to heaven, done my time in hell." The effects of all the years spent burning in brimstone were plain on Stanley's face, but his eyes were clear and filled with peace. His hair was pulled back in a graying ponytail, just like his wife's.

The Stanleys sat with Duarte and Helen Liszt in the principal's office at SAMOHI. Their son, Fabio, had been sent for and was due shortly. With the Stanleys' approval.

"Only reason I'm alive now," Jeff said, "is because of Carlene's painting. One morning I was crashing after frying my brain for so long I couldn't remember."

"Two weeks," Carlene said.

"Yeah. Anyway, the last thing I saw before I was about to pass out was Carlie painting. She was doing this floral scene.

It was so beautiful it almost made me cry."

Duarte saw Mrs. Stanley smile. Bet herself that Jeff Stanley had cried.

"I told her, the world was as pretty as her paintings, I wouldn't have to do drugs. She just took my hand and led me out to our backyard, showed me where those same flowers were growing right out of the ground. She told me right then all she did was copy things; the real artist's work was on display everywhere we went. I went into rehab that same day. My roommate was this guy who used to steal from people on TV, a televangelist. My luck was, this time he'd really found his faith. The man saved himself one soul in me, anyway."

Carlene Stanley squeezed her husband's hand.

"Of course," Jeff said, "it didn't hurt that Carlie had saved about half of what I made during my rocking days so we're still loaded."

There was a knock at the door; it opened, and Candace said, "Fabio's here."

She stepped aside and the boy stood in the doorway. Not quite as tall as his father, but getting there, and slight, as he'd been described to Duarte. Surprising her, the boy's haircut and clothes were conservative. An appearance that Duarte wished her Sebi still had. Fabio didn't seem inclined to walk any farther into the lion's den than he'd already ventured.

But his father got out of his chair and said, "Have a seat next to Mom."

The boy did as he was told.

Jeff said, "I'll go stand in front of the door, in case he makes a break for it."

Candace closed the door, leaving, and Jeff Stanley blocked it.

Fabio looked at his mother and she took his hand. Then Helen Liszt introduced Duarte, placing equal emphasis on the facts that she was both Sebastian's mother and a police officer.

The boy started to tremble but managed to look at her.

Duarte was struck by how, even in distress, Fabio's eyes radiated an almost frightening intelligence. She felt that at a glance he was figuring her out in ways she didn't know herself.

Made her feel she had to start fast while she still had some advantage.

"Fabio, when was the last time you heard from my son?"

"Monday evening."

"Did he ask you to call school and provide a false excuse for his absence?"

Carlene had to stroke the back of her son's head before he answered.

"Yes."

"Did he ask you to do that because he knew you could?"

Helen Liszt leaned forward.

"Yes."

"Do you take money for this service?"

"No ... but I ask anybody I help to donate five dollars to the school's special activities fund. You know, so the teams can get new uniforms or the band can have new sheet music."

The principal sat back, perplexed by the boy's mix of deception and school spirit.

Trying to keep her voice steady, Duarte asked, "Fabio, do you know where Sebastian is right now?"

The boy hung his head and shook it.

"Do you think he might get in touch with you?"

"Maybe. Sebi and I like to talk."

"Will you please let me know if he does?"

Still avoiding Duarte's eyes, Fabio nodded.

"Even if Sebi asks you not to, you have to let me know."

The boy's head bobbed once more.

"And you have to stop the phone phreaking. It's a crime."

Carlie put an arm around her son's shoulders, but he still shuddered.

Duarte had gone as easy on the kid as she could, spoke softly, didn't badger, hadn't asked for his accomplices' names, but there was only so much slack she could cut Fabio Stanley. There was also one disturbing thought she wanted the boy to clear up for her.

"Fabio," she said, "please look at me."

The boy raised his eyes. They were sheened with tears but Duarte still felt they could see all the way to her soul.

She said, "It's not going to be easy for you to tell your friends you can't help them any more, but you have to do it or you'll be arrested, and nobody wants that. Do you understand?"

"Yes."

"So how many students will you have to disappoint, ones you've already agreed to help. Three or four?"

Fabio Stanley's face crumpled. For the first time the boy-genius was gone and he looked like nothing more than a distraught kid.

"How many, Fabio?" Duarte repeated.

"Twenty-seven."

The number made Helen Liszt straighten up in her chair.

"All on the same day?" Duarte asked.

"Yes."

Exactly what she'd feared. A group of kids going to the

death concert, they weren't about to spend their last day alive sitting in a classroom.

"When?"

"Tomorrow," Fabio Stanley told her.

CHAPTER 20

Detective DiLeo called Valkonen and said, "Hey, Sarge, got a minute?"

Valkonen was stuck in the late afternoon crush heading west on Olympic. He told the dick to hold on and squeezed out of his lane to turn onto a side street. He pulled to the curb so he wouldn't become another idiot paying attention to his phone call instead of traffic.

As a cop, Valkonen's cast iron opinion was that traffic fines should be doubled for any driver who collided with another vehicle while blathering on a cell phone. Double the jail time for any dope who hit a pedestrian or bicyclist.

"What's up?" he asked DiLeo.

"Shanley and I haven't had any luck finding MacShane. How about you?"

"Not so far, but I do have someone else you can look for."

"Who's that?"

"MacShane's doctor." He gave them Rupert Ralph's name and connection to the UCLA Med Center. Told them about the doc's bogus excuse for disappearing after talking to MacShane.

DiLeo liked the information. "Yeah, we'll definitely add him to our list."

"Any word what killed Gregory Meltzer yet?" Valkonen asked.

"Autopsy's done but not the blood work. We're still waiting for the COD." Cause of death. "You got anything else for us?"

"Another name. Jimmy Bern, B-E-R-N."

"Who's he?"

"Wannabe music manager." Valkonen gave Bern's business address to DiLeo.

"And he's important because?"

"Gregory Meltzer was seen with him not long before he died."

DiLeo got excited hearing that; Valkonen thought he heard DiLeo's partner, Shanley, say something in the background.

"Hey, that's great, Sarge," DiLeo told Valkonen. "Another possible doer for the Meltzer kid, a more likely one. Everything we found out about MacShane tends to exonerate him. No history of violence at all. A bleeding heart, if anything. This is good stuff, Sarge."

Valkonen heard Shanley say, "Better'n we ever hoped," before DiLeo told him to shut up.

"Here's the thing, Sarge," DiLeo continued. "My partner and I, on something this big, we felt we had to take it to the chief of detectives. He felt he had to talk to Chief Barton himself. Far as we know, the two of them are talking right now. Our boss thinks this is a matter detectives should handle. Not you. But Shanley and me, we thought we should give you a heads-up, out of respect for all the work you've already put in. That way you could ease out of it on your own, defer to us voluntarily rather than be relieved. Be an easier way for you to go out; I understand you're pulling the pin soon. And congratulations on that."

Valkonen thought: Prick. He wanted to kick himself for giving DiLeo the information about Doctor Ralph and Jimmy Bern. He should've known he couldn't trust —

DiLeo asked, "You still there, Sarge?"

"I'm here. Thanks for letting me know where things stand. But you know, I'm a stubborn SOB. I'll keep going until Chief Barton tells me to stop. Himself. Not the chief of detectives."

There was a muffled debate on the other end of the call. DiLeo must have placed a hand over his phone, but Valkonen still heard Shanley call him an asshole.

Then DiLeo's voice was back in the clear.

"You'll still keep us informed on anything else you find out, right Sarge?"

"Oh, yeah," Valkonen assured him. "Absolutely."

"Tell me you were lying about sharing anything else with that pustule," Duarte said to Valkonen, after he'd told her about DiLeo's phone call.

The two of them were sipping Bass Ale and sharing an order of chips, a.k.a. french fries, at an English pub called Ye Olde King's Head on Santa Monica Boulevard. The place would be jammed in an hour but at the moment they had a corner table at a front window to themselves. Both of them were in the mood for a beer, but took care to blot the alcohol with saturated fat.

"Of course, I was lying," Valkonen said. "Question is, did they believe me?"

"Not if they got a brain between them."

"Yeah. And we sure can't expect them to share with us." Valkonen took a sip of beer and nibbled a fry. "Thing is, this shouldn't be a pissing contest. So, thinking about it, I don't feel too bad that I told them about Doctor Ralph and Jimmy Bern. Better to have four cops looking than two. Especially if this thing really is coming down tomorrow."

Duarte drained her glass, looked like she wanted another but held back. She took a pack of gum out of her handbag and popped a stick in her mouth, put another on the table for Valkonen if he wanted it.

She was staring off into space when he said, "It's a good sign Sebastian used the Stanley kid to set up an excuse. Shows he still has some concern for the future."

Duarte looked at him. "Or he did before Audra died. Maybe we should ask Marta Waldman how many kids buy into the Romeo and Juliet scene. My guess is a lot."

Valkonen could see how each passing minute was rubbing Duarte's nerves raw. It was always easier imagining bad things happening to your kid than good things. They needed to get back to work, give all the nervous energy she was building up a focus. Let her feel she was doing something positive.

"I think Jimmy Bern's the key right now," Valkonen said.

"And who's gonna tell us how to find him, Miss Cleo?"

"I was thinking Walter Thornberry at Clive's. He's the one who gave me Jimmy's name."

Duarte bit her lower lip. "Yeah, Walter might be good."

"You want to work this together or cover as many bases as we can?"

She gave him a hard look. Would've chilled most people but it heartened him.

"I still know how to be a cop, Valkonen. You work your town, I'll work mine."

Fabio Stanley had given Duarte the names of all the SAMOHI kids who'd bought "excused" absences from school for tomorrow. He'd been reluctant until she'd told him she could just check who'd donated five bucks to the activities fund, but it would look better for him if he cooperated.

She'd shared her information with Valkonen.

Now, she'd volunteered to go interview 27 suicidal kids and their clueless parents all on her own. Just what she needed right now.

"You sure you don't want me to help?" Valkonen asked.

Duarte stood up and glared at him.

"What you can do, you can pay our tab," she said. "You're the rich cop."

She walked out. Valkonen put money on the table and started to follow.

Went back and got the stick of gum Joan had left for him.

CHAPTER 21

Valkonen was just about to knock on the door at Clive's when Chief Barton called.

It took Valkonen two rings before he decided to answer. He was tempted to let his voice mail take the message. But if the chief was pulling him off the case, voice mail wouldn't be able to argue his side of things.

"Sergeant Valkonen," he said, taking the call.

"It's me, Rick," Barton said.

"Yes, sir."

"Detective DiLeo said he's spoken with you, so you know the situation."

"I know the chief of detectives is trying to grab the case."

"His men have developed some leads."

"If you mean Doctor Ralph and Jimmy Bern, I gave DiLeo those names."

There was a moment of silence. Valkonen didn't like it. So he filled it.

"Chief, if the detectives found those leads, do they have someone to talk to who might help them find Jimmy Bern? Do they know the name of the band we're looking for?"

"They didn't mention either of those things," Barton said.

"But they would have if they'd known them. To impress you. To bigfoot the case."

"You actually have that information, Rick? You're not just being clever here?"

Valkonen laughed, something not ordinarily done when a cop talked to the chief, but maybe the honesty of his reaction would help rather than hurt him.

"I'm not that devious, sir," he said. "Just a cop working the case *you* assigned me."

Of course, Valkonen was assigned before Barton or anyone else knew whether the suicide concert was anything more than a twisted joke. Now that most, if not all, doubt had been dispelled, the powers that be were obviously wondering if a single sergeant who'd spent most of his career on patrol duty, had gone on to be a babysitter with a badge, and was now working what started out as a punishment detail, was really the right man for the job.

The chief of detectives had already cast a no vote; Barton's prolonged silence might indicate he was leaning that way, too.

"Chief," Valkonen said, "I was just about to interview a person who might provide critical information. I'm literally standing outside his door. But if you want me to come in and brief the detectives, I'll do that. Then I'll put in my retirement papers immediately afterward."

Telling Barton that Valkonen wouldn't be the department's scapegoat if the dicks screwed up and everything went to hell, but the chief would be open to questioning from the media and the pols about why he'd removed the original investigating officer — one who'd seemed to be making progress.

"You have 24 hours, Rick. We'll review the situation then."

The chief clicked off.

Barton's deadline worked out just fine for Valkonen, if Duarte was right and one more day was all the time they had left. Things got hairy at the end, they'd be calling for back-up anyway.

Until then, though ... What if Barton had the chief of detectives with him when he'd made his call? The C of D's could be getting the word right now that Valkonen had information his detectives didn't. Once that nugget reached DiLeo and Shanley, they'd be calling him, reaming him for holding out on them and making them look bad.

Valkonen turned his cell phone off.

He'd check it every thirty minutes for messages from Joan.

Maybe he was a little more clever than he'd led the chief to believe.

"Walter," Valkonen said, "were you shitting me or was Mickey T. shitting you?"

Valkonen was sitting at the bar in Clive's, a glass of sparkling water in hand. Walter sat two stools away facing him, not bothering about a drink. It was four hours before opening time and they had the place to themselves.

"What do you mean?" Walter asked, looking puzzled.

"I mean, you told me Mickey T. was so sick he'd be out the rest of the week. I go to his condo, bang on the door for five minutes, and all I get is a sore hand. Didn't even hear a moan from anyone inside. You know, 'Please help me, I'm dying.' Like that."

Walter frowned and said, "What I told you is what Mickey T. told me."

"Yeah? Did he *sound* sick when he talked to you?"

Walter sighed. "Could tell you I ain't no doctor. But what it sounded like to me, he found some honey he wanted to wine, dine, and shine on after a few days. Being he's the boss, though, what am I going to say? I said, 'Get well.' I'd take care of things till he did."

Valkonen nodded. "Thanks for your honesty, Walter."

"Yeah. Hope it doesn't cost me my job."

"Better that than being an accomplice to a crime."

Walter frowned again. "Mickey T.'s too smart to commit a crime."

"Let's hope. In the meantime, I need your help finding Jimmy Bern."

"Thought you were looking for the kid was with him."

"He's been found, dead. Now, I need to find Jimmy."

Walter was still grappling with the first part of Valkonen's news.

"Someone's dead inside this thing of yours?"

Valkonen nodded. "I'm trying to hold the number at one."

He took a sip of his water while Walter ruminated.

To stir the big man up, Valkonen came at him from another direction. "When you gave me all those demo CDs the other day, Walter, I was kind of surprised I didn't find one from what I hear is the hottest new band around these days."

"Who's that?"

"Death Penalty," Valkonen said.

Walter leaned forward, like he was trying to see if he was being BS'ed.

"What're you talkin' about? That CD was on top of the stack in one a them boxes. Death Penalty is Jimmy's band, the one he manages. Probably why I thought of where I saw that kid you wanted."

Valkonen took another hit of water, searched his memory.

"When you gave me the boxes with the CDs," he said, "they were closed but not sealed."

"Yeah," Walter agreed. "Just folded shut."

"Who else had access to them?"

"Before I passed them on to you? Just —" Walter stopped abruptly.

"Maybe Mickey T. isn't as smart as you think," Valkonen told him.

Walter shook his head. "He might be in on some money dodge, I could see that. That's what the music biz is all about. But I'm telling you, man, Mickey T. wouldn't kill nobody."

"We can still hope for that. But right now, Walter, I've got to find Jimmy Bern and fast. Any help you can give me is going to help things work out better for everyone."

Walter didn't know where Jimmy lived, but he gave Valkonen a list of clubs the would-be music mogul frequented. Told him the places the hustler liked to eat.

Gave him a detailed description of Jimmy's appearance.

Two minutes later, Valkonen phoned it in to Evie for a sketch.

CHAPTER 22

Duarte cursed herself for being a prideful fool.

How the hell long was it going to take her to do 27 interviews? She'd be ringing people's doorbells in the middle of the night. Be lucky if the homeowners only called the cops or let the dogs out on her. She went to a house where somebody was just a touch unbalanced, or simply had a bad day, the resident might come to the door with a gun in his hand.

Shit. Why hadn't she been smart enough to let Valkonen help her?

He wasn't a bad guy at all. Not a caveman or a sex-hound like a lot of the cops she'd known. He was almost too nice, really. She hadn't once caught him checking out her form.

Could he really be that hung up on the woman who'd married his sister?

Talk about your unrequited love.

Duarte took out her phone and called him. Grimaced when she got his voice mail. What kind of a dummy cop wouldn't have his phone on when … Jesus, was Valkonen avoiding a call from his chief? Was it really possible he could be yanked off the case right when the whole thing was about to come crashing down?

Crashing down on her. All by her lonesome if Valkonen got recalled. Damn!

She told Valkonen's voice mail, "It's me. I changed my mind. Let's work together." Then she added, "Those dopes on LAPD pull you off the case, I'll make you my ride-along, okay? Just call me. Soon as you can."

CHAPTER 23

Valkonen checked his voice-mail two minutes before Duarte's message came in. Doing so, he thought checking for calls every thirty minutes was maybe a bit obsessive. Joan had been pretty tense when they'd parted company. He doubted she'd call anytime soon. So he bumped up the interval for checking his voice-mail to every hour.

Be easier to keep track of that way.

The clubs Walter had listed for him as Jimmy Bern's hangouts were clustered close enough to reach on foot. Many of them were places he and Joan had already visited. He walked up one side of Sunset and down the other. Only at the last place on Walter's club list, a dingy joint he and Joan hadn't hit, did anyone respond to his banging. The character who opened the door was a real puzzle to Valkonen. He couldn't tell if the emaciated person under the black t-shirt and jeans was male or female. Or for that matter alive or a zombie. Unevenly chopped green hair with red roots stood on end. Chalk white skin stretched tight across hollow cheeks. Lips as black as the t-shirt and jeans formed a gash beneath empty gray eyes.

"Yeah?" the creature asked tonelessly.

"Cop," Valkonen replied, showing his badge. "I'm looking for a guy named Jimmy Bern. You know him?"

"Unh-huh."

The affirmative grunt perked up Valkonen.

"He's not inside, is he?"

The kid shook the green-and-red-haired head.

"You mind if I look?"

"For Jimmy? Go ahead."

"What's your name?" Valkonen asked.

"Peggy Sue."

"Should've guessed," he said. "Got tired of the pigtail look, huh?"

Peggy Sue smiled. Her yellow teeth had been filed to points. She held the door open for Valkonen. The inside of the club was as dark as a grave. Being the gentleman he was, Valkonen insisted Peggy Sue go first.

Even taking that precaution, he flicked on a light switch he noticed inside the front door. It turned on a strobe light. Made Peggy Sue dance into and out of sight. Not reassuring at all. Where the hell was Duarte when he needed her?

"Come on," Peggy Sue said. "I don't bite. Well, yeah, once or twice I did."

Valkonen told himself even with those teeth of hers he could take a 90-pound vampire. He searched the club, including the unisex john, which was lighted with red bulbs. Satisfying himself no one else was present, he returned to the front door.

"Done?" Peggy Sue asked.

"You know what Jimmy's up to?" Valkonen asked.

"About five-six."

Ghoul humor. Still, it was good to know the guy's height.

"I mean the concert."

"Yeah, I heard."

"With Death Penalty."

"Great band."

"You know where it's going to be held?"

Peggy Sue shook her head.

Valkonen tried to spot a lie but Peggy Sue didn't so much as blink.

"You know how many kids are going?"

"A lot, Jimmy said."

"But not you?"

"Unh-uh."

"How come?"

Peggy Sue told him, "I died a long time ago."

CHAPTER 24

Duarte discovered that the suicide concert wasn't the only game in town that week or even first on the list of things to do for many of the teenage set. What really had their hormones revved was a little get-together some of them had planned. Seemed a lot of kids were avid fans of a cable TV series on the doings of ancient Rome. In the fashion of others who liked to relive moments from the past, a group of the local high schoolers had decided to reenact a Bacchanalia, the Roman festival honoring the god of wine, Bacchus. Giving things a modern twist, there would be other drugs besides alcohol, but there would be plenty of group sex and other historically accurate party diversions.

All of this information came courtesy of a 16-year-old who styled herself after the show's rendition of Agrippina, the scheming second wife of the Emperor Claudius.

Agrippina got Claudius to make her son by a previous marriage, Nero, his successor. Nero not only wound up fiddling as Rome burned, he had Mom killed when she got on his nerves.

Despite all that, the girl fancied herself as the empress.

Her real name was Ardris Michelman. Her father was a cosmetic surgeon, her mother a jewelry designer. Their combined incomes would have done noble Romans proud.

"Where were you planning to have this little shindig?" Duarte asked.

"Right here," Ardris said. "We'll start early, while there's still dew on the grass."

"Un-huh," Duarte responded. She and the empress were seated on facing love seats in the Michelman's living room. Mom and Dad looked on from perpendicularly placed easy chairs. "You still planning to carry on with things then?"

"Why shouldn't we?" she asked.

Duarte looked at the parents, offering them the opportunity to jump in.

It took them longer than it should have, to Duarte's way of thinking.

Dr. Michelman assured Duarte, "We'll have a long talk with Ardris."

"A long, *stern* talk," his wife added.

Duarte saw the empress roll her eyes.

She told Duarte, "Daddy's off to Chicago first thing tomorrow to receive an award for building better boobies. Mom'll be in the limo with him to catch her flight to New York to talk to a department store chain about carrying her designs. Do you think worrying about me is going to keep either of them home?"

Duarte made a point of not looking at either parent.

"What about me?"

The kid smiled. "What about you?"

"I'm a cop. I know. You told me about a party featuring drugs and underage sex."

"Oh, that," Ardris said mildly. "I lie all the time. And whatever happens, you won't be able to see it from the sidewalk or even if you peek over the garden wall. So what reason would the police have to enter private property?"

Duarte nodded. "You're pretty good."

The empress deigned to give a nod to the plebeian.

"You've got things figured out so well," Duarte said, "you have no reason not to tell me who's on the guest list."

"None whatsoever."

The empress fetched her school yearbook. She sat beside Duarte and pointed out the pictures of who the revelers would be. Good looking kids, every last one of them. Duarte ticked their names off the list Fabio Stanley had given her, counting as she went.

A frown crossed her face. "Including you, I count 19 people: ten girls, nine boys. An odd number."

The empress's eyes gleamed. "Don't worry. No one will be left out."

Duarte had heard enough. She stood and looked down at Ardris.

"Call your friends and tell them the party's off. Tell them to show up for school tomorrow."

The empress laughed at her. "Or what? You'll tell their parents? They won't care any more than mine do."

"I'm not thinking about anyone's parents," Duarte told her. "I'm thinking about cops. The ones who'll be posted around this property five minutes from now. The ones who'll pick up any kid who shows up here tomorrow as a truant."

Duarte looked at Doctor and Mrs. Michelman and then back to Ardris.

The girl's eyes were now slitted in rage. Didn't faze Duarte one bit.

She said, "You want to skip school, that's between you and your parents."

Following up on her threat, Duarte called the SMPD's top kiddie cop from her car parked at the curb in front of the Michelman house. The place was built in the fashion of a Mediterranean villa. Apt setting for a Roman orgy, she thought. But not this time.

Not with a bunch of underage kids.

No matter how overprivileged they were.

She told the lieutenant in charge of youth services what had been planned at the Michelman house for the following day. Suggested it wouldn't look good for the department if the little shits actually pulled it off. Informed the lieutenant she would pass the info along to SAMOHI's principal so she could make sure the kids all showed up at school tomorrow.

The last bit, about telling Helen Liszt, insured that the lieutenant couldn't deny that Duarte had informed him in a timely manner. He didn't stop the Bacchanalia, it was on him not her. Might've been a little paranoid on her part, but when you were a pariah in your own department, you couldn't be too careful.

It surprised Duarte to realize she felt more vulnerable without Valkonen around.

Why the hell hadn't he called back, anyway?

She picked up the copy of the most recent SAMOHI

yearbook that Helen Liszt had given her. With the elimination of 19 of the 27 purchased school absences at one go, she'd made a big jump on her interviewing task. Maybe she wouldn't be out all night after all.

Duarte looked at the pictures of the remaining eight kids on the list Fabio Stanley had given her: one freshie, three juniors, four seniors. No sophs.

Except for her Sebi. More than ever, she was sure Valkonen had been right. With Sebi's girlfriend dead, he was going to be at that goddamn concert.

The best reason she had to stop the damn thing.

She returned her attention to the pictures. Four boys, four girls. She flipped back and forth between the pictures. At first, she thought it was her imagination, but checking and rechecking she saw it was more than that. Not so much that they looked alike, the boys and girls, but for each one there was another who looked right for him or her. In her mind, Duarte paired them off. Four couples. She'd bet her badge on it. For these kids, suicide had been a joint decision, a way they thought they could carry on their love beyond this life.

The dumbasses. She really had to prevent this madness.

But over the course of the next hour she learned that none of the eight was at home. In each case, they'd told their parents they'd be studying at a friend's house, staying overnight.

Only none of them was where they said they'd be.

They were all missing.

CHAPTER 25

Valkonen swung by Evie's house before he went to check out the places Jimmy Bern liked to eat. He told himself that was the smart thing to do. He could pick up the sketch of Jimmy that Evie would have ready by now. He could also pick up the Death Penalty CD. Listen to the music, see if it gave him any ideas.

Most of all, though, he once more felt a compelling need to see Jack.

Maybe hold him on his lap, tickle him, even roughhouse a little.

After leaving Peggy Sue, he couldn't help thinking, or at least hoping, that at one time she had been somebody's little girl. A gift from God. Maybe she had worn pigtails a year or two. When she'd been Jack's age with a gap-toothed smile. Not filed teeth gone yellow.

His thoughts hadn't stopped there. He tried to picture what circumstances had brought Peggy Sue to where she was now. In her own words, dead a long time. Must've been some horrific form of abuse, sexual or psychological. Or both.

Jack, on the other hand, was loved and nurtured by every adult in his life.

But even for Los Angeles, Jack's life was hardly normal. He got to his teens, he'd have a lot to rebel against if the mood took him. And the way the world was going, Valkonen couldn't imagine what vices might be available to him if he did assert himself.

He pressed the doorbell at Evie's house, listened to Beethoven, and saw a small hand pull back the gauze curtain at the glass panel beside the door. Jack peeked out at him.

He called out with a giggle, "Who's there?"

"Police, buddy," Valkonen said gruffly. "Open up!"

"Are you gonna arrest me?"

"Have you broken the law?"

"I didn't eat my peas tonight."

Valkonen laughed. He hated peas, too.

But he said, "You'll get five years of going to bed early for that."

"No fair!"

"Okay, if you let me in right now, I'll see if the judge will go easy on you."

The door opened and Valkonen grabbed Jack up into his arms. He raised the boy over his head and tickled his belly with the top of his head. He stopped as soon as he heard what sounded like Jack's dinner coming up on him.

"You okay?" he asked, holding Jack in his arms.

Jack burped and said, "Sure."

"Where are Evie and Dana?"

"Right here," Evie said. "Me, anyway. Dana went to talk to her nieces and nephews. She's ... concerned. Wants to make sure they stay close to home for a while."

"Good idea," Valkonen replied.

"Mommy Evie drew another picture for you, Dad."

Dad. Jack took both adults by surprise with his casual use of the word. Valkonen held the boy close and looked at his sister. He saw that she was touched, and a little frightened.

Valkonen looked at his son.

"Jack, I want you to always remember something."

"What?"

"No matter what happens, I'll always love you. So will your mommies. We will always help you in any way we can."

Jack said nonchalantly, "I know." He kissed Valkonen on the tip of his nose and then squirmed out of his arms. "Can I have some ice cream now?"

Evie said, "A little. I'll get it for you so a little doesn't become a lot." She took Jack's hand and looked back at her brother. "The sketch is on my art table."

Valkonen went back to Evie's studio. He saw the drawing and picked it up.

Looking at it, he said, "Gonna get you, Jimmy Bern. In time, too."

Then it hit him — the sketch and time getting short reminded him.

He'd forgotten to see if Joan had called him.

No sooner had he turned his phone on than it rang. He answered before looking at the caller ID. It wasn't Duarte; it was Chief Barton.

Valkonen's heart sank, sure he was about to be relieved of the case. Forget the 24 hours of grace.

But the chief told him in a brittle voice, "Rick, my sister just called me."

Valkonen didn't understand. "Your sister in Vermont?"

"Yes, it's Justin and Justine." The chief's twins.

"What about them?"

"They went on a field trip, a school thing. They —" The chief had to clear his throat. "They got on a bus this morning. Went to Boston. But when it was time to go back home, they were missing. The Boston PD's got every available cop looking for them. But I —"

"You think they've come back here," Valkonen said. "To go to the concert."

CHAPTER 26

Chief Thomas Barton of the Los Angeles Police Department made the trek west to Santa Monica to speak with SMPD Chief of Police Marletta Moses. To Barton's credit, he wasn't the type of guy who felt the head of a much smaller department, and a woman at that, owed him the deference of showing up on his doorstep. Barton had been a street cop for ten years, had survived three shootouts, and had presided over four police departments around the country with budgets in the hundreds of millions of dollars. His ego was secure, and he was smart enough to know that extending simple courtesies to his fellow chiefs won him an enormous amount of goodwill when he needed a favor.

He brought with him to the conference room at SMPD headquarters on Olympic Drive his chief of detectives, Amos Mackey, who in turn brought DiLeo and Shanley.

There they met with Chief Moses and her chief of detectives, Elgar Wist.

The main links between the two departments on the matter at hand, Valkonen and Duarte, were seated next to each other at the large oval table.

The two chiefs spoke briefly in private, needing only a few minutes to come to a working arrangement. Before they spoke to their subordinates, Chief Moses called Duarte over for a personal word. Valkonen saw his new partner nod vigorously in response to what her chief had to say. Then she returned to Valkonen's side.

Barton spoke first to the assembled group, providing the background on the suicide concert and the progress made on the case thus far.

"Most of what we know at this point," he summed up, "is the product of efforts by Detective Joan Duarte of SMPD and Sergeant Richard Valkonen of LAPD. The two of them have put aside any jurisdictional concerns to try to avert a tragedy the likes of which our cities have never seen. Detective Duarte and Sergeant Valkonen will be the examples of cooperation which we will all follow. They will also continue to be the lead investigators on this case by mutual agreement between Chief Moses and myself."

Valkonen and Duarte kept their faces expressionless.

DiLeo and Shanley, Mackey and Wist had a harder time masking their feelings. But they chose not to voice them. Their resentment, however, was not overlooked.

Chief Moses addressed the possibility of hard feelings. "As we understand the situation, time is short. Valkonen and Duarte know this case the best. They'll lead the way. If that bruises anyone's precious feelings, too bad. Follow their directions. Don't even think of freelancing. You won't like the consequences. Is everyone clear on this?"

The two chiefs of detectives and DiLeo and Shanley all nodded. Minimally.

The strong words were a mixed blessing, Valkonen thought. Barton and Moses had turned the tables on him and Duarte. Things went to hell now, they would definitely be the scapegoats. Which, from an organizational point of view, made perfect sense. Who would the two chiefs have to sacrifice if an angry public declared heads must roll? Someone valuable? No, just a guy with one foot out the door already and a broad with a bad temper.

Barton told Valkonen and Duarte, "Okay, it's your show."

They handed out copies of Evie's sketch of Jimmy Bern to everyone in the room.

"This is Jimmy Bern. He's our first priority," Valkonen said. "We find him, we'll know where this concert will be held. According to a source I located, it will have to be a pretty big venue because a lot of kids will be coming. Whether they'll all follow through and commit suicide, we can't say."

Duarte passed out paired copies of the photos she'd clipped from the SAMOHI yearbook. "These are the pictures and names of eight Santa Monica High School students we believe will be in the audience. I've paired these photos because I have a hunch these boys and girls are couples and might be found together, but that's all it is, my hunch."

Chief Moses added, "Detective Duarte's instincts have a history of being accurate."

Duarte made sure she didn't react to the compliment.

Valkonen added to the list of names of people they would be looking for: "Ian MacShane of KDSW. The station is sending a headshot of him. It should be here soon. Michael Telephus, a.k.a Mickey T. He's the manager of a club called Clive's on the Sunset Strip. His assistant, Walter Thornberry, will provide a publicity photo of him. And Doctor Rupert Ralph, Mr. MacShane's doctor. There's a photograph of him on file at the UCLA Medical Center, where he's employed.

"These people are of secondary interest because they may or may not know where the concert is to be held. Any questions?"

DiLeo nodded. "You raise an interesting question, Sarge. What happens if a kid goes to hear the music but doesn't want to croak himself? You got any ideas about that?"

It was the same question Justin Barton had asked him, the one that got the investigation started in the first place. The chief's son had wondered if it would be like Jonestown.

Valkonen answered, "If the people behind all this don't mind killing themselves, I think we have to assume they won't mind killing somebody else."

Valkonen and Duarte, by Barton and Moses's dictate, would continue looking for Jimmy Bern. Mackey and Wist would decide which of their detectives would look for MacShane, Mickey T., Rupert Ralph, and the eight missing students from SAMOHI.

Barton brought Shanley and DiLeo over to Valkonen; Duarte took the opportunity to go talk to Marletta Moses again.

"Tell him," Barton said to the two detectives.

"The blood work results are back on Gregory Meltzer," DiLeo said. It plainly hurt him to have to give up the information. "Overdose, self-administered. Prescription drug. Mother's little helper. That's the M.E.'s verdict."

Valkonen frowned. "What about the gunshot in the wall with no gun found?"

"Yeah, well, that's another mystery, now isn't it?" Shanley asked.

Everyone waited for Valkonen's reply.

"Guess it is," he said.

Wouldn't be any love lost now between him and the two dicks. Having done their distasteful deed, they turned to go. But Valkonen told them to wait.

He said to Chief Barton, "Sir, if you don't mind, I have a special task for the detectives here."

The chief asked what that was.

"I think Detectives DiLeo and Shanley should be assigned the job of finding Justin and Justine, assuming your children have returned to town."

Barton agreed and the two dicks looked like they'd been gutshot.

Valkonen had just taught them not to screw with him. Maybe sealed their fucking fates. They let the chief's kids die, they might as well eat their guns.

After they departed without another word, Barton asked Valkonen if he was going to need anything else from him.

Valkonen nodded. "Yes, sir. A couple dozen of the youngest looking cops we have. Smart ones. We find this concert, we may need to put some ringers in the audience."

CHAPTER 27

Valkonen hadn't lied to DiLeo and Shanley when he'd said he didn't know what happened to the gun that had been fired at Gregory Meltzer's house, but as soon as he and Duarte got into his car, he figured it out.

"Ian MacShane took the gun," he said.

Duarte had no idea what he was talking about. "What gun?"

Valkonen told her.

"How do you figure MacShane has the gun?" she asked.

"We agree that he knew his grandson was Waldo, right?"

"Yeah. So?"

"Knowing that and knowing we were looking for Waldo but not telling us, what would MacShane do?"

"Go see the kid. Talk to him. Find out if he planned to kill himself, and if he did, talk him out of it." That was how

Duarte saw it.

"But if he got to the Meltzer house too late, found the kid dead on the floor, the gun next to him, the picture of his parents shot up, he's going to pick up the gun."

"Wait a minute. Why didn't the kid just use the gun to kill himself?"

A gun was a cop's preferred means of suicide. Valkonen wondered if Joan had ever considered — He chased the thought away before it could show on his face.

He said, "Poison's easier."

Duarte reflected on the matter. "It's *neater* anyway. Doesn't leave as big a mess for someone else to clean up."

"Poison's more certain, too, if you use enough."

They'd both seen photos of would-be suicides who'd shot themselves in the head only to grossly disfigure themselves and remain alive. Usually with a serious loss of cognitive and motor function. It wasn't a subject either of them cared to dwell on.

"So what're you saying," Duarte asked, "the kid really was pissed at his parents?"

"Maybe without Mom and Pop even knowing it. My first thought was Gregory got along with his parents, hadn't messed up any part of his house except his room. If he respected boundaries, I thought someone else must've killed him. But if the M.E. says he committed suicide, maybe his room was a pressure cooker. Shooting the picture was his way of giving his parents the finger before he went."

"So then what, MacShane comes in after the deed is done? He starts to tidy up the scene, but leaves the shot-up picture? Seems inconsistent."

"If he only wanted to spare the parents' feelings, yeah."

"What other reason would he have for taking the gun?"

Valkonen said, "At the benign end of things, he didn't want anyone else to find the gun and put it to bad use."

Duarte could buy that. "Okay, what's the other end of things?"

He glanced at Joan and said, "MacShane needed a gun and he found one."

She chewed on that, didn't like the taste, but found it digestible.

"One last thing," Duarte said, "why did the kid do himself at home instead of the concert?"

Valkonen sighed. "Maybe he just couldn't wait to die."

He started the Z and pulled away from the curb.

Aeneas Terry, station manager at KDSW, opened the door to the MacShane-Waldman house for Valkonen and Duarte. He led the two cops back to the kitchen where Valkonen made the introductions.

"Marta's in bed," Terry told them. "She told me to go home, but I didn't think she should be alone. Not with Ian gone, and after those two detectives came by and told her about her grandson killing himself."

DiLeo and Shanley spreading cheer wherever they went.

"Fact is," Terry continued, "I tried to persuade her to check herself into the hospital. But she refused. The woman's a psychiatrist, you'd think she'd know it was in her best interest."

"We all run stop signs," Duarte said. "One way or another."

"Ain't that the truth? I made some coffee so I can stay awake. Would either of you like some?"

They both did. Without direction, Duarte immediately

found the cabinet with the cups and saucers and put them out. Valkonen managed to find the fridge all on his own and brought a carton of cream to the table. Terry fetched the coffee and spoons. The sugar was on the table.

Having sat and sipped, Joan said to Terry, "You'd have mentioned it if Ian had stopped by, right? Or if he called, you would have heard."

Terry put his cup down and said, "No visitors, no callers."

Valkonen asked, "There a computer in the house?"

"Ian has a laptop. I've e-mailed him here when he's worked from home."

"Have you seen it?"

Terry thought about the question, shook his head.

"Not in here or the living room or the guest bathroom. The only places I've been."

"But you've seen more of the house on other occasions," Duarte said.

"Yes, I've had the tour, Detective."

"Does Doctor Waldman have a home office with a computer?"

The station manager raised his eyebrows and nodded.

"Now that you mention it."

"Did Doctor Waldman say anything about using it since you've been here?" Duarte asked.

"No."

The two cops looked at each other; the station manager watched them.

"Wouldn't do to leave a stone unturned," Valkonen told his partner.

"No way," Duarte agreed.

They turned to look at Aeneas Terry.

"We came here to ask Dr. Waldman if she'd heard from

her husband," Valkonen said. "If we wake her up, how distraught do you think she'll be?"

Terry said, "I think she'll be groggy, possibly unreliable if you ask her questions. She took some sleeping pills."

"How many?" Duarte asked.

"Two. I asked her to take them in front of me so I wouldn't worry. She did. I put the bottle on the top shelf of the cabinet behind you, Detective. Out of reach. And with her sore ankle, I don't think Marta will be up to much climbing."

Valkonen liked the way Terry didn't get ruffled by Duarte's question.

"Okay," Duarte said, her tone indicating the question was justified.

"If Marta's not clear-minded," Valkonen told Duarte, "even if we wake her up, get her permission to check her e-mail, a court might shit-can the search."

"You think we've got time to worry about that?" Duarte asked.

"Just saying. Saving the kids comes first, sure. But prosecuting somebody afterward might go out the window."

Aeneas Terry interjected himself into the discussion.

"I appreciate that you took me into your confidence, Sergeant Valkonen. I'd have a hard time living with myself if I'd been sidelined in this matter and couldn't help Ian and Marta. So maybe I can return the favor. As neither of you has solicited my help, I wouldn't be acting as a police agent if I took it upon myself to look at Marta's e-mail."

"No you wouldn't," Valkonen said.

Duarte seconded the idea, raising her opinion of Terry.

"Let's go," the station director said. "I'll show you where Marta's office is."

Dr. Waldman's desk was close to the door of her office.

Her computer had a large screen monitor. Aeneas Terry turned it so the two cops didn't have to enter the room to see what was on it. Terry pulled up Marta's e-mail — and there was a message from her husband.

But all Ian MacShane said was: *Not to worry. Right as rain. Home tomorrow.*

CHAPTER 28

"Not a lot of help," Valkonen said as he and Duarte drove back to SMPD headquarters. Duarte was going to pick up her car, go home for a minute in the hope Sebi might have e-mailed her. She hadn't checked her computer on her last stop there. Then she'd rendezvous with Valkonen. Work out some sort of plan to search for Jimmy Bern in Santa Monica.

Amos Mackey was assigning LAPD dicks to run down the list Walter Thornberry had given to Valkonen of the places Jimmy liked to eat in L.A.

"We don't even know for sure MacShane's still alive," Duarte said. "Somebody else could've picked up that gun at the Meltzer house and sent that e-mail in his name."

Valkonen saw his partner was slipping into despair again.

"Marta wakes up, she'll know if it was him," he said. "You

can't fake the way someone talks to his wife."

"Yeah, I suppose you're right."

Valkonen almost said she'd know Sebi's words if he'd e-mailed her. But he didn't because who knew if the boy had. Or ever would.

Valkonen was sure of one thing: He'd need more coffee if he was going to stay up all night. He thought of a place that made a decent cup and decided to swing by before he dropped off Duarte, see if it was still open.

What he saw, what both of them saw, as the car turned the corner of Third Street, above Wilshire, was a marquee.

The El Dorado Theater.

A huge old-time rococo movie palace, the kind that had prevailed before everything went multiplex. Place hadn't been open for years. The overhead was too high these days for just one screen to carry a place that big. For some reason, though, it had never been torn down.

Valkonen pulled to a stop out front. All the doors were boarded up.

A sign said the El Dorado would be demolished ... the day after tomorrow.

The day after the concert.

Valkonen and Duarte looked at each other.

"Gotta be," he said.

"Gotta," she agreed.

Duarte sat behind the wheel of Valkonen's Z, now parked a block up Third from the El Dorado, and said she'd be back in ten minutes.

"Call me if something happens. I'll come right back," she said.

"Go check your computer, Joan. See if Sebi e-mailed you. Don't run any stop signs."

"I want to be here if—"

"If I was worried about Jack, I wouldn't give a shit about anything else."

"You're right," she said. "But call me, damnit, if anything happens."

"Will do."

Valkonen was pleased that she didn't jackrabbit the start, but moments after she turned the corner, he heard a shriek of rubber and knew a good bit of his Michelins had been left on the streets of Santa Monica. Oh, well. Dana could probably figure a write-off for him.

He looked down the street at the defunct theater. Not another soul in sight. Santa Monica went to sleep early on weeknights. He wondered if he should call for backup. Decided it was too soon. Really, all he had to go on was a hunch. What better place to hold a suicide concert than a venue that was going to be knocked down the next day? It had the kind of perverse symmetry that would get played up in news coverage. The publicity of the damned.

Fit right in with the sensibilities of a group called Death Penalty.

He and Joan should have listened to the band's CD by now. Might have given them a better fix on who they were dealing with. That or turn them into pod-people.

Valkonen thought it might be a good idea to get a look at the backside of the El Dorado. With the front all boarded up, a rear entrance had to be where everyone was going to enter the theater. Unless there was some kind of underground access, through a utilities tunnel or something. Wouldn't that be a pisser? A way for the band, a thousand kids, and assorted extras to slip inside without anyone noticing.

They could already be inside for all he knew. Five hundred couples, maybe, if Joan's take on things was right. Holding hands. Professing love that would endure beyond their abbreviated life spans. Christ, it wasn't hard to imagine.

He walked past the opening of the alley at the far end of the block. Didn't turn his head. Sneaked a peek out of the corner of his eye. His peripheral vision was good enough to tell him two things: There were no people in the alley and no obvious hiding places for him to use as a lookout.

He could, of course, simply walk down the alley and inspect the situation in a forthright manner. He was a cop. He had a gun. There was no reason to be afraid. Not for his own safety anyway. But if someone involved with the concert came along as he was rattling a door, he might blow the whole thing. Alert the suicide crew that they'd been found out. Force them to reschedule and relocate. Put the hunt back to square one.

Doubtful he'd be a lead investigator in that case.

And Joan would never let him hear the end of it. Or never talk to him again.

One of the two.

Despite all that, he felt compelled to see whatever there was to see at the back of the theater. If it seemed unpromising, then he'd check for any means of underground access. Or maybe the audience was going to chopper in.

That last thought was fanciful, but it gave Valkonen an idea.

He walked quickly along Second Street, parallel to the back of the El Dorado. He stopped about 200 feet from the corner. That would put him, he hoped, approximately opposite the near rear corner of the theater. He looked at the building in front of him. Two stories with the ground floor occupied by a storefront acupuncturist's office. Doctor Yeh. Trained in China. Professional motto: Bring the Pain. Upstairs was an apartment. A sign on the door to a staircase leading to the second floor said the apartment was for rent. There were no lights on upstairs or down.

No one strolling down this street, either, a quick look showed.

Duarte would like what he was about to do, Valkonen thought.

Being as quiet about it as he could, he kicked in the door to the stairway.

It was easy. Place needed better locks. The apartment door was no better. Two minutes later Valkonen was up on the building's roof, peeking over the parapet at a slight angle to his left at the backside of the El Dorado. Telling himself he was taking a terrible risk. Had actually committed the crime of breaking and entering. Be a terrible thing if it cost him his pension.

All of his concerns vanished when he saw Peggy Sue appear at the mouth of the alley. Strange as L.A. could be, he didn't think there were two people in town, alive or dead, who looked like her. She stopped in front of a door at the back of the theater. Used the index finger of her right hand to count over one, two, three, four bricks at shoulder height.

She pulled out the brick, stuck her left hand in the space and came out with a key. She used it to unlock the back door. Replaced the key and the brick and went inside. Presumably relocked the door from in there.

Sonofabitch, Valkonen thought, Peggy Sue was ratting him out.

If she had no personal interest in suicide, that was the only explanation.

She'd lied to him when she said she hadn't known where the concert would be held and Valkonen, having no experience interrogating zombies, had bought it. Now, she was down there reporting that the cops might be closing in.

And who might Peggy Sue be talking to?

Jimmy Bern?

Valkonen would bet Jimmy was in the theater right now.

He called Duarte.

CHAPTER 29

Wednesday

Duarte got back fast, just after midnight, and did what was probably the right thing, even if it wasn't what Valkonen thought they should do. She reported in to Chief Moses. Which meant Valkonen had to call Barton. Which meant dozens, if not hundreds, of cops were on the march. No, on the move. SoCal cops drove, didn't walk. But forces were gathering.

And would soon catch up to the lead investigators.

Valkonen and Duarte were not on the roof of Doctor Yeh's building. Valkonen didn't want to include Duarte in his crime. Nor did he want to implicate himself. His pension was too important to his future. He'd smeared the footprints on the doors he'd kicked in and wiped down the few surfaces he'd touched inside the building.

The two cops were back in Valkonen's Z with him behind the wheel, parked a half-block up from where Peggy Sue had entered the alley. They'd seen no sign of anyone else arriving at or leaving the El Dorado.

"We're going to look like horses' asses, if we've called out a horde of cops and no one's in there but Peggy Sue," Valkonen said.

"You're the one thinks Jimmy Bern is inside."

"Yeah."

But Valkonen was no longer so sure. What if the derelict movie house was only the place where a lost soul like Peggy Sue could climb into her coffin for the night?

"You also said maybe the whole audience is already in there, waiting patiently for the show to start. Remember that?" Duarte asked.

"Now that you mention it." But Valkonen wasn't so sure of that either. A big crowd would need restrooms, and he didn't see the El Dorado's plumbing as functional.

"Besides all that," Duarte said, "I've got to be straight with Marletta."

The SMPD chief.

"Yeah?" Valkonen asked.

"She pretty much was all that kept me on the job when I slugged that creep."

"Your chief of detective's didn't back you up?"

"Elgar Wist? Not a big fan of women in the workplace. Thinks he should be chief."

"Ah," Valkonen said. He gave it a moment and then asked the question he'd been avoiding, "Any e-mail from Sebi?"

Duarte shook her head. "Not from Sebi, no."

Valkonen said, "Somebody else?"

"Fabio Stanley. He wanted me to know how badly he feels about Sebi skipping out on me. He says he'll help me look for him. Community service for his misdeeds."

"Always good to see remorse, but how's he going to help?"

"He didn't say, but I didn't give him my e-mail address and he found it anyway, so maybe he has ways."

"Could be." Valkonen hoped so.

"There was a call on the phone machine, too," Duarte said. "Helen Liszt at SAMOHI."

"The principal?"

"Yeah. I called her about that orgy I told you about. You know what that little brat who planned the thing did after I told her I'd have cops posted around her house?"

"She moved it to someone else's house," Valkonen said.

Duarte gave him a look. "Yeah. So whose house was the backup?"

"Her best friend's. The principal figured it out. Maybe went to see both girls."

For a moment, Valkonen thought Duarte might slug him, but her shoulders slumped and she told him, "You're a pretty good cop."

Except when it came to finding her son, Valkonen thought. He didn't have time to dwell on that. His cell phone, set to vibrate, gave him a small jolt.

"Sergeant Valkonen," he said, answering the phone.

"Everyone's in place, Rick," Chief Barton told him. "You and Detective Duarte have three minutes. If I don't hear from you by then, we will be coming in hard behind you."

"Yes, sir." Valkonen wanted to know just how hard. "Any news on your twins, sir?"

"Negative." The troops would be coming hard indeed.

"The count starts now."

Valkonen and Duarte got out of his car and ran down the alley behind the El Dorado. Valkonen found the hidden key quickly. He slipped it into the lock, looked at Duarte and saw her nod. He turned the key and threw the door open.

CHAPTER 30

Duarte charged into the El Dorado with her gun drawn. With her forward lean, she was sent flying when somebody or something tripped her. In the light from the alley, Valkonen saw her land hard and skid into darkness.

He didn't want to make the same mistake Joan had made, but he couldn't wait to help his partner. Yet wait he did. Didn't dare move an inch.

Because without seeing how it was done, but hearing a terrifying *hiss*, someone put a long, sharp blade to his throat. And someone else jammed a gun against his head.

The cavalry would arrive in only a minute or so.

If he and Duarte had that much time left.

He was pulled inside, the door was kicked shut, and bright lights went on. The harsh illumination blinded Valkonen for a moment. His hearing, though, was unimpaired and he heard a familiar voice. One with a British accent.

"Sergeant Valkonen," the voice said with a note of surprise.

The blade was withdrawn from his throat, the gun from his head.

Duarte asked, "You okay, Rick?"

Valkonen ran the fingertips of his left hand under his chin. The rest of his face bore a day's growth of beard. But the skin under his fingers had been shaved smooth. Couldn't come any closer than that to having your throat slit.

He lowered his hand and said, "Yeah, I'm fine. You?"

His eyes were adjusting; he saw that Duarte had picked herself up and put her weapon away. She was dusting herself off.

"I'm fine."

"Terribly sorry, Sergeant," Ian MacShane said. "We thought you and Detective Duarte were someone else."

We consisted of MacShane and Mickey T. The former college fencing champion was sheathing a samurai sword. A third man, wearing a stethoscope around his neck, looked on without speaking. Dr. Rupert Ralph, Valkonen presumed.

"We'll get to that in a minute," Valkonen said. "I've got a call to make."

He called Barton and told him all was well. Cancel the combat assault. At the chief's insistence, he and Marletta Moses and an appropriate number of gun-bearers would be coming in. Valkonen said he'd open the door.

Holstering his own weapon, he did so.

He told MacShane and company, "These guys coming in will be on edge for a minute, so don't do anything foolish."

MacShane relinquished his gun to Valkonen. Mickey T.

laid his sword on a table.

Valkonen, unable to stop himself, rubbed the underside of his chin again.

Jimmy Bern and Peggy Sue were tied, torsos and legs, to chairs placed on the stage of the El Dorado. The bodyguards for the brass had been dispensed with and MacShane spoke to the four cops who remained in the theater, Valkonen, Duarte, and the two chiefs.

"In its heyday," he said, "the El Dorado hosted live music acts, big bands, as well as cinema performances."

Barton focused on police matters. "Are you holding these people against their will?"

"Citizen's arrest," Mickey T. told him.

Jimmy Bern tried to protest, but he'd been gagged.

Peggy Sue hadn't; she just sat silent with a thousand-yard stare.

"So you were about to call the police," Chief Moses said, "and transfer your prisoners to the proper authorities."

"Yes, well, as to that —" MacShane began.

"We tried to call Sergeant Valkonen and Detective Duarte," Mickey T. said. "You can check my phone records. I was told Valkonen was on special assignment and nobody knew how to reach him. Detective Duarte, for some reason, doesn't seem to be too popular with her colleagues. I was told she'd get my message, but I never heard back from her."

"There are lots of other cops you could have talked to," Barton said.

Mickey T. just shook his head.

MacShane elaborated, "Intending no offense, sir, but your department and police organizations in general are not known for their delicacy or finesse."

"How delicate do you have to be to arrest someone?" Barton wanted to know.

With a sweep of his arm, MacShane gestured to the thousand seats in the auditorium, "How would you arrest so many young people, each of them bent on self-destruction. If you swooped down on such a crowd, you'd be lucky to take half of them alive."

Chief Moses said, "So we keep them from gathering here."

"And they find somewhere else to put on the show," Mickey T. said. "Or they kill themselves in smaller groups. To make the cops look bad, if nothing else."

Valkonen could see that. So could Duarte.

"So what's your idea?" Valkonen asked.

"Let the fans enjoy the show and then before they can make their fatal mistakes show them just how dreadful death can be," MacShane said.

"And how are you gonna do that?" Duarte wanted to know.

Mickey T. told her, "I'm gonna chop a kid's head off."

The kid's name was Woodrow. He wasn't real — only a Hollywood animatron — but Valkonen thought he looked a lot more normal than Peggy Sue, right down to his sullen expression and blotchy complexion. Could pass for, say, 17 to 20. He even had one hand holding on to the back of his oversized pants to keep them from falling to his ankles.

Still, from a distance of five feet or less, you could see Woody wasn't human.

"You're not going to let anyone in the audience get too

close," Duarte said.

MacShane smiled. "We'll have help there. Death Penalty takes serious umbrage with anyone trying to climb onstage with them."

Mickey T. explained, "There are stories they've kicked in the teeth of kids who've tried it. We're going to control the lights, too. Woody will look plenty real, his head will drop into a basket, and a gallon of what looks just like blood will shoot out of his neck."

"Woodrow will also struggle and moan a bit before he gets the chop," MacShane added.

"That's supposed to do it?" Valkonen asked. "Or are you saying the plan is for Mickey T. to threaten to cut off everyone's head?"

Mickey T. shook his head. "That'd be over the top. But you're close."

"Just tell us, okay?" Duarte said, getting impatient.

MacShane told them. The guy with the stethoscope, an actor named Geoffrey, not Doctor Ralph as Valkonen had thought, would stand at the entrance door with a couple of bruisers. Geoffrey's name tag would identify him as Doctor Death. Each person admitted would be relieved of any guns, knives, and toxic agents he might possess. In return, he'd be given a placebo and told it was poison — so everyone would share the same death experience.

Except for the members of Death Penalty. As showmen, they had to die far more dramatic deaths. They were the ones who would be put to the sword.

"They've agreed to be decapitated?" Duarte asked, skeptically.

"What Jimmy told us," Mickey T. said, "was that they asked to be surprised."

"The information is to be withheld from them until the last note of music is played," MacShane said.

"Let me see if I understand this," Valkonen said. "You tell the boys in the band they're going to lose their heads and Woodrow will show them what they've got coming?"

"Exactly," Mickey T. answered.

"Why Woody?" Duarte asked. "How'd he get picked to lose his head?"

"The poor lad is a volunteer from the audience," MacShane told her.

"Won't the band members see he's not real?" Valkonen asked.

"As you can see, this stage is big enough to accommodate literally dozens of musicians. There are but four in Death Penalty. Woodrow is to have his own little corner far from the others."

Mickey T. said, "We're betting nobody's going to crowd in for a good look."

"We're also wagering," MacShane said, "that Death Penalty won't follow through on their commitment to die young."

"And if they don't, the audience won't," Valkonen said. "Unless some kids try to, and pop their placebos. Which will give away the whole con."

Mickey T. just grinned.

MacShane said, "Yes, well, we've given that matter some thought. Dr. Death will explain from the stage that while the poison he's passed out is usually quite reliable it doesn't work for everyone every time."

"Yeah, but don't worry," Mickey T. said, "because if you only get a headache, I'll come by to finish you off."

MacShane concluded by telling the four cops, "So you

see, ladies and gentlemen, we're trying not only to stop a horrible situation in the near term but also firmly implant the idea that taking one's own life is something never to be considered. Of course, whether we're allowed to proceed is now entirely up to you."

CHAPTER 31

Valkonen and Duarte had no say in the matter. For that matter, neither did Barton. The scene of the potential crime was in Santa Monica, but returning Barton's earlier deference, Marletta Moses consulted with him. Out of earshot of the others. It took them maybe two minutes to come to a decision.

They called their lead investigators over to them.

"It's not going to happen," Barton told them. "Not like those two had it."

"It's a crackpot idea," Chief Moses added.

Their subordinates nodded. Didn't venture to speak.

"You do agree, don't you, Detective?" Moses asked.

She bit her lip, then said, "My son's missing. I was hoping he might show up at the concert and I could find him. In time, you know."

"And you, Sergeant?" Valkonen's boss asked.

"The plan is risky, no doubt, sir. They think they've got things covered. But in a situation like the one they've got in mind, something always goes wrong. They let the kids keep their lighters and smokes, they could set the place on fire. Wind up killing everyone anyway."

The two chiefs exchanged a look. Valkonen had conjured a nightmare that hadn't occurred to them. "Good point, Sergeant," Chief Moses said.

"Thank you, ma'am. But Mr. MacShane and Mr. Telephus also raise important considerations. We can stop things in the short term, but if we don't change a lot of hearts and minds we're just delaying the inevitable."

"So what's your idea, Sergeant?" the L.A. chief asked.

"I wish I had one, sir."

"Maybe I do," Duarte said. "Maybe I do, after all."

They needed Jimmy Bern's help to make Duarte's plan work. First, though, they had Peggy Sue taken away by paramedics. She might have been catatonic for the lack of response she showed to being placed on a gurney and rolled away. Valkonen wanted to reach out and squeeze her hand, but that wouldn't be a part of the role he was playing. It was just him, Duarte, and Jimmy onstage now. Jimmy was still tied to his chair and gagged.

Duarte removed the strip of cloth and the small rubber ball that had been used to silence Jimmy. He hacked up a wad of phlegm and spat it out, taking care not to hit either cop. Then he tried to speak, but his throat was too dry. Providing water would have eased things for him, but putting the punk at ease wasn't part of the deal.

As Jimmy recovered, his eyes darted back and forth between Valkonen and Duarte.

Finally, he asked, "Which one of you's the good cop?"

Duarte pinched his nose shut, put the ball back in when he opened his mouth.

"I am," she said. "My partner's the bad cop. Get him pissed, see what happens."

Jimmy's eyes bugged out.

Valkonen looked at Duarte. "He's scared. Must mean he doesn't want to die."

Duarte said, "That right, Jimmy? You don't have suicide in your future?"

The kid shook his head vigorously.

"Because you're not crazy, are you?"

Jimmy indicated he wasn't.

"I take the ball out again, you gonna show us any more attitude? 'Cause if you do, I'm gonna turn things over to my partner."

Tears welled up in Jimmy's eyes. Duarte took that as a sign of concession. She removed the ball. Waited a moment for Jimmy to relubricate his mouth.

"Okay, Jimmy," Duarte said, "here's the deal. You just admitted that you don't intend to kill yourself. Said you're not crazy. Means you're of sound mind. So that means you're an accessory to what could be the deaths of hundreds of people. How much time in the joint do you think that's going to get you? Till you're dead and your bones turn to dust, that's how much."

"DA might find an angle to impose capital punishment," Valkonen offered.

Duarte smiled. "The death penalty for killing Death Penalty. Poetic."

Jimmy looked like he was about to swallow his tongue and save everyone the trouble.

Duarte leaned in close to the boy. "Such a shame. We saw the recording and video equipment you've got here. You were gonna make the biggest live album ever, weren't you? Really put you on the road to riches. Make you a legend."

Tears seeped from Jimmy's eyes. Tears of regret.

"So how'd you like a shot at having at least some of that?" Duarte whispered.

Jimmy tried to see if she was fucking with him. Then he dared to hope and nodded.

"Cause there might be a way out for you, Jimmy, if you do *exactly* what I tell you."

Jimmy's response came out as croak. "Anything."

Duarte led Jimmy away. Took him outside. He hobbled, his legs stiff from all the time spent sitting tied to the chair. Valkonen waited in the theater. A moment later, Ian MacShane joined him.

"Detective Duarte said you wished to see me, Sergeant."

"That's right, Ian, I do. Turn around, place your hands on the wall, and spread your legs."

"I beg your pardon."

"Do it," Valkonen ordered.

"Are you arresting me? On what possible char—"

Valkonen spun the radio personality around and pushed him up against the wall. Holding him there with his left hand, he quickly frisked him with his right. He found the gun — a single-shot derringer — in the right hip pocket of MacShane's pants

"On an illegal gun possession charge, Ian," Valkonen said.

He took his hand off the man, told him to turn around.

"How did you know?" MacShane asked.

"You took the gun Gregory used to shoot the picture of his parents. I had to ask myself why. At first, I thought it was to intimidate, if not shoot, somebody else. But then you told us about using Woodrow to show everyone how awful dying could be. Maybe you could have pulled that off, maybe not. If not, a smart guy like you would have a back-up plan. Your medical history suggested what that might be."

MacShane lowered his eyes.

Valkonen continued, "But what would you use to kill yourself? You gave me the gun you took from Gregory. Turned it over with no fuss at all. So maybe you had a backup."

Valkonen glanced at the small weapon in his hand.

"Jesus, Ian, do you really think shooting yourself is a sui-cide-prevention tool?"

"Must be a sort of madness that runs in the blood. Poor Gregory." He looked up at Valkonen and blinked twice. "You won't tell Marta, will you?"

Valkonen sighed. "You put Doctor Ralph on standby for her, didn't you? In case, you ..." He raised the hand holding the derringer. "Your no-worries e-mail to Marta was just a ruse."

"I'm not quite sure what it was. Self-delusion perhaps."

"I'm going to have an officer take you home, Ian. You're going to check yourself into an appropriate treatment facil-ity. I imagine part of your therapy will be telling your wife what you were thinking about doing. My condolences on the death of your grandson."

MacShane nodded. Then he said, "If you're going to allow the concert to go on in some fashion, I really would like to see it."

"Come anywhere near it, Ian," Valkonen said, "and I will arrest you."

CHAPTER 32

Duarte's idea was to pull the same stunt that Ardris Michelman, the wannabe Roman empress, had tried to pull with the orgy she had planned: switch locations at the last minute. Doing that, contacting all those who would be in attendance at Death Penalty's farewell performance, was possible because Jimmy Bern, whatever his other faults, was highly organized. Made Valkonen and Duarte glad he had the music biz as a career goal and not terrorism.

The El Dorado wasn't the only site for the concert that Jimmy had arranged, even though it was his first choice, with a stage, the theater environment, and the planned demolition the following day. It was perfect.

But also acceptable was a vacant warehouse directly under a flightpath into LAX. The roar of jets landing would cover the sound of the music and provide suitably punk

accompaniment, ear-splitting noise, to the band's composi-
tions. A third site was a canyon north of town which featured a small natural amphitheater. The setting was maybe
too pretty a place for a mass suicide, but it had the advantage
that the entrance was narrow and could be dynamited shut.
Creating that good old nobody-gets-out-alive feeling.

Except for Jimmy, his sound engineers and videogra-
phers.

Oh, they were supposed to go, too, but Jimmy had per-
suaded Death Penalty that he and his crew had to be the *last*
to die. So they could create the record of everyone else's
demise.

Yeah, sure. As Jimmy told Valkonen and Duarte, "You're
not a dipshit; you know the music business is all about lying
and being lied to."

What really surprised the cops was that Jimmy had the
names of everyone he expected to attend the concert, all 513
of them. Including Justin and Justine Barton, the chief's
twins. But no Sebastian Duarte.

Sebi's mom asked him, "How'd you do this? Make this
list."

"Passed the word on the street. Everyone who wanted in
had to provide a name and a phone number. That and the
reason they wanted to die. I checked backgrounds on the
Internet. It's gonna give the video a documentary feel, you
know?"

"And you decided to let the chief of police's kids in?"
Valkonen asked.

Jimmy shrugged. "Makes a better story, doesn't it?"

Valkonen decided Jimmy would either die young or run a
major record label someday.

"What about crashers?" Duarte asked. "Kids who hear

about it from someone on the list and decide to tag along?"

Sebi, she meant.

"We've got room for extras," Jimmy told them.

"But you haven't told anybody yet where the concert will be held?" Valkonen asked.

Jimmy shook his head. "For security." He laughed at himself. "Guess I coulda done a better job with that, huh?"

The two cops just stared at him.

"So how the hell are you supposed to let people know where to go?" Duarte asked.

"Do a flashmob," Jim said. "I make a call. That person makes three. Those people each make three, and so on. Doesn't take long and the cellular structure limits knowledge."

Little shit was feeling smug, Duarte thought. She liked him better bound and gagged.

Valkonen looked at her. "The warehouse for the existing audience?"

"Yeah, I think that's what the chiefs would want."

Jimmy eyed them. "So I make the call and then I'm cool?"

"You make the call and then one more thing," Duarte said.

"What?" Jimmy asked, anxiety edgy back into his voice.

Made him much more likable.

"Tell you in a minute," Valkonen said. "For now, just sit quietly right where you are."

Jimmy was in the backseat of a patrol unit. The two cops got out and moved a few feet away. Far enough that he couldn't hear them talk.

"You're gonna go to the warehouse?" Valkonen asked Duarte.

"Yeah."

"Sebi could still show up," he told her.

She nodded tightly.

When she looked at Valkonen he could see how afraid she was.

"Sebi comes your way, he's your first priority, right?" she asked.

"You're my partner, Joan. What do you think?"

She nodded again, her anxiety eased not at all.

CHAPTER 33

The way the cops worked it at the warehouse was a hybrid of the MacShane-Telephus plan and the kind of sting law enforcement liked to use with mopes who had outstanding fugitive warrants. When the audience for the concert showed up, they were met at the door by a crew of four young plain-clothes cops. All of them bruisers. All of them dressed and accessorized to look more like bikers than guys who wore badges.

They patted down everyone who entered to make sure they weren't armed or carrying their own toxins. One of the team, a guy who was good with numbers, kept a running count in his head of the number of people admitted. The guys on the door took away 23 firearms, including a flare-gun, 56 knives, 18 straight razors, and over 2,000 pills from those who intended to overdose.

In return for the confiscated items, each person was given a black capsule. So everyone could share the same death experience, they were told.

Most of the audience was under 30, but middle-aged and retirement rockers were also represented. Gender breakdown was roughly 60-40 female to male. In appearance, most of the audience was well-fed and cleanly dressed, but there was a significant fraction that was unbathed and ragged.

Interestingly enough, every last person seemed sober. Some were strung out, but nobody arrived already stoned.

The cop counting noses told Duarte 509 people had shown up. Four fewer than Jimmy Bern's expected number. She wondered if the four had come to their senses ... or if, like Gregory Meltzer, they'd been unable to wait.

Once inside, people took seats on metal folding chairs. Unreserved seating. To keep the right vibe, a badly shot video of an earlier Death Penalty performance was shown on a big-screen projection TV placed in the middle of a makeshift stage. And a countdown clock let the audience know just how long they had to wait until the show went on.

All this was taken from the fugitive-sting handbook. Get all the suckers gathered together in one secure spot — more commonly with the promise they'd won tickets to a big sporting event — keep them happy for a while, and then spring the trap.

In this case, though, one twist was added to the normal procedure. At the five-minute mark in the countdown, two lucky people were selected at random to go backstage and say hello to the band. Those two fortunate souls just happened to be Justin and Justine Barton.

The twins were still missing when the clock expired, the

big-screen TV was pushed aside, and a figure stepped out from behind the curtain that had been rigged across the stage. Detective Joan Duarte walked up to a microphone stand. She scanned the audience side to side and front to back before she spoke.

Then she said, "Sorry to say, Death Penalty can't be here. But in their place, we've got another group for you: The Police."

The curtain opened to reveal not Sting, Stewart Copeland, and Andy Summers, but a uniformed line of L.A.'s finest. There was a moment of stupefaction before a significant part of the audience make a break for the doors. Their way was blocked by more cops.

A majority of those present, however, sought a more permanent exit. They popped the black capsules they'd been given. They were, of course, placebos, but they dissolved quickly releasing a purple dye would stain the tongues of those who'd ingested them, and thereby identify attempted suicides, for the next 48 hours.

The police intended to use the mere presence of those in the audience at what had been billed as a suicide concert as possible grounds for involuntary commitment to mental health treatment centers. The purple-tongued people would go to the head of the line.

No mention of Chief Barton's kids being present would ever be made.

Sebi Duarte never showed up.

CHAPTER 34

Though they never introduced themselves onstage, Death Penalty consisted of Kaz Bannis, lead singer, lead guitar, and songwriter; Trevor Bannis, rhythm guitar and cousin of Kaz; Mingo Rix, bass; and Seferino Linares, drums. Their amps, mikes and drums were already set up onstage at the El Dorado. The band was behind the curtain with their manager, Jimmy Bern.

"How many people we got out there?" Kaz asked Jimmy.

"About 250 or so," Jimmy answered.

"That's all?"

"Price of admission is pretty stiff."

"Stiff," Mingo laughed, an edge to his voice, "that's good. What we'll all be soon enough."

"Shut up," Kaz told him.

Mingo didn't argue. Nobody in the band argued with

Kaz. It was his group. He formed it right after he got out of the Division of Juvenile Justice facility he was sent to for beating a kid into a coma. The kid, at age 15, had made the mistake of trying to steal Kaz's guitar from the garage where he composed. While Kaz was awaiting trial, the kid's brain function ceased and he was put on a respirator. The D.A. tried to persuade the family to pull the plug so he could charge Kaz with homicide as an adult. But the family held out hope, at first. After they had the time to reconsider, they liked the idea of Kaz being executed and pulled the plug. But by then Kaz had taken a plea deal and been convicted and sentenced as a juvenile on a charge of aggravated assault.

The kid he had beaten died the week after Kaz started serving his sentence.

His counselor brought Kaz the news. In California, it was hoped, however foolishly, that juveniles could be rehabilitated. Kaz's counselor, though, was a realist. He knew which of his boys would graduate to adult confinement and told them so. To the worst of them, he said, "You've got death penalty written all over you."

He'd told Kaz exactly that. Gave Kaz the name for his band. Not that Kaz ever gave his counselor the satisfaction of saying so, he agreed with him.

He would get a needle stuck in his arm someday. Unless he took care of things first. The thing to do, as he saw it, was to make a name for himself, make the world look up to him, beg him for more of his music, then give everyone the finger, and off himself.

And take as many people as he could with him.

Thing was, he'd exhausted his gift fast. The songs he wrote were fueled by his rage, but just being pissed off was a limited source of inspiration. He started to repeat himself.

Anybody taking a critical look at his work would see that, and they'd start slamming him for it. Shitting on his rep. It'd be much better to go out on top.

As for the other guys in the band, they were weak. High school dropouts. Marginal musicians. Without him, they wouldn't get a gig playing a carwash opening. Shit, they'd be lucky to get work *in* a carwash. They'd wind up in the joint or sleeping under a freeway. They were better off dead, too.

"What'd you come up with, Jimmy?" Kaz asked. "How we do ourselves in?"

"Thought you wanted it to be a surprise."

"Yeah, I do. But it better not be anything pussy. No pills."

"No pills."

Kaz stared hard at Jimmy. "You know what I don't see when I look at you?"

"What?"

"Fear. I don't see any fear. My boys here, they're all scared. They'll do what I tell them; they know I'm smarter than they are. Know what's good for 'em. But they're still scared. You aren't."

Jimmy laughed. He was starting to feel scared.

But he said, "Took a Valium or two so I could do my job, that's all."

"Yeah, your job. Maybe I should choke you out right here."

"Won't get your video that way." Jimmy was good and scared now.

Kaz wanted to leave a record of his farewell-and-fuck-you performance behind. He wanted people to remember him, argue about him for long time. Maybe start fights and spill a little blood trying to decide if he was better than the next hot-shit act to come along.

He also liked the way Jimmy was shaking just then.

"Who's that old fuck over there behind you?"

Jimmy knew who he meant. Didn't have to look.

"Videographer."

"I'm supposed to believe someone like him's gonna kill himself?"

"He's got lung cancer. Nothing to lose."

Kaz laughed. "Goddamn, Jimmy, you *do* know how to pick 'em." Then he leaned in close to the band manager and whispered, "But just in case you happen to change your mind about dying yourself, I put out a hit on you. You might last 24 hours, but that's all."

The creative force behind Death Penalty laughed again, grabbed his guitar, and strode onstage. His mates followed on his heels.

An ashen Jimmy Bern turned to look at the old fuck videographer.

Valkonen, with a camera on his shoulder, recorded his terror.

There were exactly 250 civilians in the audience. Jimmy Bern had recruited them on a moment's notice. It was easier in beachfront Southern California than it would have been most places. There were always people on the streets who didn't seem to be bothered with the necessities of going to work or school. The crowd at the Death Penalty concert was probably a bit older, on average, than the one sucked in by the cops' sting. Better dressed in general, too. Better looking even. Definitely happier.

No prospective suicides, as far as anyone knew.

In addition to the music lovers, there were two dozen

plainclothes cops. None was over 28 years old. All were bright-eyed and steel-spring fit. They blended perfectly.

Stage chatter played no part of a Death Penalty performance. Even song titles weren't announced. You had to figure things out for yourself. The guitarists plugged in; the drummer settled in behind his kit and picked up his sticks; and they were off. They started with "Anna Phylactic's Shock." It told the story of a girl who plans the perfect murder of an abusive boyfriend, pulls it off over a picnic lunch, and then just as she's about to flee the scene of the crime gets killed by a bee sting.

Valkonen hated to admit it, as he recorded the performance from his spot at the side of the stage, but he found the lyrics morbidly amusing, and the music was great. Hard driving guitars, throbbing bass, banging drums. Reminded him of a cross between the Kinks and the Who, back in their early days. The singer's voice wasn't great, and the band's musicianship was ragged, but those glitches probably could have been overcome if Death Penalty had intended to live longer.

The audience, however, had no quibbles at all. They roared their approval. Three other videocams, besides Valkonen's, got crowd and band shots.

Kaz's reaction to the wave of approval was nil, but his bandmates grinned.

Without delay, Kaz launched Death Penalty into "Soap on a Rope." This was the recounting of a fish — a new inmate at a youth facility lockup — taking his first prison shower. It wasn't pretty. In fact, it was horrific. But, damn, if the music didn't work perfectly with gruesome lyrics. Built the tension and compelled you to listen right through to the bloody end.

Little sociopathic fucker has talent, Valkonen thought, as he zoomed in on Kaz's twisted smile at the end of "Soap."

The concert continued without pause for the next 11 songs. The band worked hard, leading the audience through a tour of hell that would have made Dante upchuck. Most of it had to with prison life, such as "What're You in For?" and "Waitin' on the Needle." The former was a bragging session of the crimes committed by six young inmates, each trying to top the others, before they all ambush and kill a counselor. "Needle" followed those involved in the murder: one rats out the others; four use every available legal avenue to prolong their lives; and one admits his guilt and says execute me, but plans to kill himself before the state can do the job.

By now, Valkonen was trying, not always with success, to ignore the hooks and riffs of the hard rock music. He was concentrating on the lyrics, the monstrously twisted points of view of the band as voiced by its lead singer. The cop in him was coming to agree with the idea the world would be better off if these punks did kill themselves. Have their CDs and videos reduced to plastic slag and dumped with the band's human remains into a toxic waste site.

Valkonen's thoughts made him smile inwardly. He was getting as bad as Kaz. He told himself to keep his attention as focused as his videocam. Just stick with the plan.

Death Penalty machine-gunned through their first 13 songs in fifty-five minutes.

Finally, they took a breather. Mopped the sweat from their brows. Kaz pulled a bottle of vodka from his guitar case, took a deep pull, and passed it to his mates. The people in the audience all looked like they could use a drink, too. The music they'd been battered by had them pumped with adrenaline; the images that had been conjured for them had filled their minds with dread.

After what seemed like all too short a respite, Kaz spoke to the crowd for the first time. "Okay, you fuckers, this is the last song, and then we get serious."

Unlike all the other songs, "No Reprieve" started soft and slow, showing a range of expression that was completely unexpected. Looking through his view-finder, Valkonen paid close attention. He'd been surprised by Kaz having the vodka with him; he had to watch out for anything else the punk might have smuggled into the theater.

"No Reprieve" was a postcard to the devil from his son. Kaz claimed there was no need for a blood test to prove paternity. The proof was in a lifetime of misdeeds. The prodigal would soon be home. And when he arrived, they'd see who could raise the most hell. The pace and intensity of the music built, but there were rests, brief at first, growing progressively longer, in which the instruments fell silent, and the bass player, Mingo, provided a deep, diabolical, chilling laugh. Until at the end, Kaz's hands fell from his guitar, his right hand, formed the shape of a pistol, which he pressed against the side of his head. Just as his thumb, representing the gun's hammer, fell, Seferino, the drummer, slammed a stick against his snare drum producing a crack like a gunshot .

Kaz collapsed, a metaphorical bullet to the brain.

In the background, Mingo laughed and laughed and laughed.

Nobody beat the devil.

The audience sat in stunned silence for the better part of a minute. Then it erupted into sustained applause. Valkonen kept his focus on Kaz, who got to his feet to even louder applause. He tolerated it for a minute and then cut it off with an electronic shriek as he stomped on his guitar, purposely left on the stage.

"That's enough of that shit," he yelled.

The audience bowed to his command and fell silent.

Mingo was no longer laughing. He and Trevor and Seferino looked terrified.

Kaz paid neither them nor the audience any attention. He looked to his right for Jimmy Bern, who was supposed to be waiting in the wings, just behind Valkonen.

"Okay, Jimmy," Kaz said, "whatever you've got, let's have it now."

A Smith & Wesson .38 slid across the stage floor and stopped at Kaz's feet.

A Police Special. Kaz got the joke. He picked up the revolver with a smile.

"Suicide by cop's gun, huh, Jimmy? That's not bad." Holding the weapon casually at his side, Kaz turned toward the audience. "I don't know how you fucks are planning to kill yourselves; we're using a gun."

The audience's silence deepened. They weren't sure of what they were seeing, but they were hoping like hell it was all part of the act. As Kaz turned his head toward his bandmates, he failed to notice several young men and a few young women creeping toward the stage.

Kaz looked at his friends — Trevor and Mingo still holding their guitars, Seferino crouched behind his drums — and asked, "All right, boys, who wants to go first?"

He extended the gun in their direction.

Valkonen put down his camera, but he didn't draw his own weapon.

Trevor, Mingo, and Seferino all looked at each other, waiting to see if anyone would actually step forward. None did. If anything, they all tried to make themselves small behind their instruments. Their moment had arrived and they were found wanting.

"You punks!" Kaz sneered.

He wanted to shoot them all himself, but homicide wasn't the point.

Unless they all killed themselves, how could they expect the jerks in the audience to do the same? And if he killed himself first, he was damn sure those other chickenshits wouldn't. They were making him look bad. With the goddamn cameras catching it all.

"You fuckers," Kazz hissed. He had to single one of them out. "Trevor, you're family. Show 'em somebody's got some balls around here."

Trevor started to cry. He only clung to his guitar and shook his head.

Kaz's face turned so red it looked like he might die of a stroke.

By now, everyone in the audience knew this wasn't an act. A murmur of fear rippled across the theater. Kaz swung his head. Partially misread what he saw. A lot of those useless fucks out there in the seats had started to move toward the back of the theater. More goddamn cowards. But other people were coming his way. Guys with the balls to do themselves in; some chicks with spine, too. Good to see he wasn't alone.

Valkonen now stood 10 feet behind him.

Kaz looked at his drummer and bassist. "What about you guys?"

He pointed the gun their way.

Seferino Linares threw his drumsticks at Kaz.

Prison reflexes kicked in and Kaz shot at him. He didn't see how he missed, but Seferino got away. Kaz turned to

Mingo and Trevor who were rooted where they stood.

A woman in the audience cried out, "No, don't!"

But Kaz did. He fired two shots each at Mingo and Trevor.

Trevor went down, but Kaz was pretty sure he just passed out. Mingo remained paralyzed but upright. There wasn't any blood anywhere. Kaz just could not understand how he'd missed all five shots.

With only one round left, he knew he had to kill himself now. Inspire the fools who were crowding the stage and they would follow his example. He turned back to look at them and saw ... every last one of them had a gun pointed at him.

Not regular guns. Tasers. They weren't planning to kill him, themselves, or anyone else. That was when Kaz finally got it. The whole thing was a setup. He'd been conned.

Well, fuck them all, he thought. He couldn't miss his own goddamn head. He stuck the barrel of the .38 in his ear and —

The gun went flying from his hand as Valkonen tackled him from behind.

Wouldn't have mattered if Kaz had pulled the trigger.

All the rounds in the gun were blanks.

EPILOGUE

Kaz Tannis was charged with three counts of attempted murder, one count of conspiracy to commit murder, for the hired hit on Jimmy Bern, and one count of attempted suicide. He was confined in the Los Angeles County Medical Center Jail Ward. His court-appointed defense attorney wanted Kaz committed to the state hospital for the criminally insane, which would relieve Kaz of the responsibility for trying to gun down his fellow band members. The D.A. argued that Kaz's plan to have Jimmy Bern killed showed he was rational and, as he refused to name the killer he'd hired, remorseless.

The judge in the case decided to keep Kaz in the Jail Ward pending a battery of examinations by both prosecution and defense experts. Just to be careful, Kaz was kept on 24-hour suicide watch.

Involuntary confinement of the mentally ill in California

was contingent upon a person being suicidal, a danger to others, or unable to scrounge for food and clothes. In the event that Kaz's mental state bought him a walk on the criminal charges, it seemed likely his actions would qualify him for a prolonged stay in a locked ward. Provided the personnel doing the suicide watch didn't get sloppy.

On the other hand, some of Death Penalty's fans asserted that, California being California, he would be confined just long enough to gather the material for a great new album.

Trevor, Mingo, and Seferino all grew affluent, if not rich, from the success of "Anna Phylactic's Shock" becoming the most commercially downloaded song of the year and later a movie of the same name in which, Hollywood being Hollywood, there was a surprise ending with Anna killing the bee instead of vice versa.

The three members of Death Penalty who were at liberty were renamed The Sellouts by music critics who battered them for profiting off of Kaz Tannis' creativity and not having the gonads to kill themselves.

Jimmy Bern defended Trevor, Mingo, and Seferino, saying he'd drawn up the agreement stating that all four members would share equally in any profits the band made, less Jimmy's 25% commission, of course. Kaz, anticipating his future to be brief, had gone along with giving away the fruits of his labors. Jimmy said he was putting Kaz's share of the money into T-bills for him to redeem if he was ever again a free man.

Which was a lie: pure music industry BS. Jimmy was using Kaz's share to hunt for the hitman Kaz had sicced on him. Kaz was intent on causing Jimmy grief? Fine, the cost of fixing it would come out of Kaz's pocket. If Kaz ever got out of the nut house, he was going to be penniless. Jimmy was going to be living in a guarded estate. Let's see Kaz get to him then.

Jimmy figured he'd dole out the other Death Penalty songs little by little to keep the name profitable as long as possible. The way he saw it, the remaining three nitwits from Death Penalty would overdose, crash their motorcycles, or fall off hotel balconies, leaving him with all of the band's money.

Only thing was, he did have to keep watch for Kaz's damn hitman. The killer might have a sense of professional pride. He might wait for Jimmy to let down his guard and then blow his brains out. So while Jimmy was sure he was on his way to fame and fortune, he never could stop looking over his shoulder.

Ian MacShane retired from his job at KDSW. Hearing that he'd contemplated another suicide attempt, Marta didn't commence another round of psychotherapy, she simply gave her husband a choice: her or rock 'n' roll. MacShane saw immediately that she wouldn't accept anything less than an immediate decision. He wisely chose her. They relocated to Marta's native Vienna where their home was filled with flowers and the music of Mozart.

But before he left Santa Monica, MacShane donated four decades worth of rock memorabilia to KDSW to auction off during its next pledge week. The treasure trove would raise $5 million for the NPR station. The amount would be sufficient to rate a plaque bearing Ian MacShane's name, likeness, and a biographical note to be placed in KDSW's lobby.

The former rock journalist never got to see it.

Mickey T. one-upped Jimmy Bern by buying the rights to Death Penalty's farewell performance video from the LAPD for $1 million plus 10 percent of all monies from all sources of exploitation that the video might earn. Gross points from the first dollar. L.A. cops knew better than to take net points. They had the right to audit Mickey T.'s books monthly, too.

For a brief moment, Jimmy Bern thought to contest this arrangement unless he and the band members were properly compensated for the video. But he quickly dropped his claim. There were rumors that Mickey T. had paid Jimmy a visit, and had brought along his samurai sword.

Nobody needed two guys looking to kill him.

Rick Valkonen retired from the LAPD with his pension benefits locked in and then was rehired as a lieutenant. Impressed by Valkonen's success, Chief Barton didn't want to lose his services. The agreement Barton struck with Valkonen was that Valkonen would work solely and directly for him. No other police official could impose his authority on the new lieutenant. Should one try to do so, Valkonen was free to tell him to get lost.

In addition, Valkonen would be promoted to captain two years hence. The increases in rank and duration of service would be reflected in Valkonen's final pension from the department. All of which meant, with Dana's canny investments, that the beach house Valkonen eventually bought should be a lot nicer than he'd ever hoped.

The agreement would terminate in five years, the longest either man could see continuing to be a cop in Los Angeles.

Valkonen was in the midst of two weeks vacation, having spent the first week with Evie, Dana, and Jack in Honolulu, giving his son surfing lessons in the gentle waves of Waikiki. He planned to spend the second week with Joan Duarte, maybe sleeping on her sofa if she said she didn't want to be alone.

Sebi had never shown up at either Death Penalty venue. Nor had he contacted Joan's brother or her parents. The Duarte family had gathered during the week Valkonen was in Hawaii, trying to decide what they should do. What they could do.

Valkonen pushed Joan's doorbell, hoping deeply that he might be of some comfort to her. He was buzzed in without a query as to who was at the door. Maybe she'd seen him enter the building, Valkonen thought. He could imagine her sitting at her window watching the street.

Watching for years maybe.

The door to her unit was open when he arrived.

Valkonen called out, "Hey, Joan, it's me."

She'd been commended by her department, too. Bumped a grade in rank. And given compassionate leave time.

"Come on in," her voice came back to him. "Close the door, okay?"

Valkonen did as he was instructed. Moving into the apartment, he saw her sitting, as he'd guessed, at the window. She was wearing dark shorts and a sleeveless white top. She looked like she'd lost weight in the week he'd been away. There was lean muscle evident, to be sure, but she looked

like she hadn't been eating much.

Made him glad he'd brought his gift.

He held up the box for her to see. "Chocolate macadamia nuts."

He half-expected her to reject them, but she said, "Open the box and bring 'em over."

He did, and carried a chair from the dining area table so he could sit with her. She took three of the nuts, looked at him and said, "Nice tan."

She ate the nuts, grinding them hard between her teeth. To be sociable, Valkonen took one for himself. Joan reached over and grabbed three more.

"Should've brought more," she said.

"There's another box in the car."

They were quiet then, looking out the window, for the better part of an hour.

Finally, Joan looked at him and said, "What I think happened?"

"Yeah?"

"I think Sebi brought Audra out of the ocean after she drowned, posed her body to give her some dignity, and then went right back in, swam so far out he could never make it back, and just ..."

Strong as she was, she couldn't bring herself to say it.

Valkonen took her hands in his. She didn't pull away.

"My dad said no, Sebi'd never do that. My mom, too. Eugene, I think he agrees with me."

"I'm so sorry, Joan."

She looked at him. "So you're on the thumbs-down side, too, huh?"

Before Valkonen could answer, the phone rang. Joan held on to his hands.

"Let it ring," she said. "I don't want to talk with anyone now."

The machine picked up on the fourth ring and the voice that came out made both of them turn their heads.

"Ms. Duarte, you there? This is Fabio Stanley."

Valkonen and Duarte looked at one another. She squeezed his hands harder.

"I found him, Ms. Duarte. I found Sebi."

She released her grip on Valkonen and jumped from the chair. She had the phone in her hand a heartbeat later. "Where is he, Fabio?"

Please don't let it be a morgue, Valkonen prayed.

"He did *what?*" Joan asked.

Sounded serious to Valkonen, but not fatal. She ran back to the window. Valkonen turned to look out. They saw him at the same time. Sebi Duarte. In cuffs. Being marched home by two Marines wearing sergeant's stripes. A Marine officer walked at the head of the formation.

"Yes, they're here, Fabio. Thank you, thank you so much."

Tears flowed freely from Joan's eyes as she ended the call. She told Valkonen, "He joined the Marines. Lied about his age. Had some fake IDs. Said he wanted to serve in combat."

The doorbell rang and Joan buzzed the callers in.

"Fabio found Sebi," Joan continued to Valkonen. "He called him, and when Sebi refused to come home, Fabio ratted him out to the Marines. What a great kid."

Valkonen was overjoyed, but he was sure Joan's reunion with her son would be far from smooth sailing. He had a difficult decision to make here, so he punted.

"You want me to stay or go?" he asked.

"Stay. Please, Rick, stay. Grab me if I'm about to say or do something stupid. Don't let me go too far with my boy, not the minute I get him back."

There was a knock at the door. Joan ran and opened it. She darted past the surprised Marine officer and embraced her son. "Oh, thank God!"

The Marines had the manners to give the mother and son a moment.

Then the officer said, "Ms. Duarte, may we come in?"

She stepped back and extended her arm in welcome. As Sebi stepped past, it hit Joan for the first time that her handcuffed son might be in some kind of serious trouble. What had he done? She was just about to ask when the officer anticipated her.

"Your son enlisted fraudulently in the Marine Corps, Ms. Duarte."

Getting her bearings back, Joan said, "That's *Detective* Duarte, Lieutenant."

"I stand corrected, Detective. Your son defrauded the United States government of expensive training services."

"Can't be the first time that's happened."

"No, ma'am. The Corps is quite experienced with the situation. As we are with the reasons many young men enlist under duress. When we were alerted to your son's case, we did a routine check with the local law enforcement agencies. Sebastian Duarte is wanted for questioning by the Los Angeles County Sheriff's Department regarding the drowning death of a young woman named Audra Stevens."

Joan's eyes narrowed. "Did you question my son regarding this matter?"

"No, ma'am. The JAG officer who reviewed the case decided that was best left for the civilian authorities."

"Then why didn't you bring my son to the sheriff's

department?"

The Marine lieutenant looked uncomfortable.

"Per the agreement made with the informant who revealed your son's fraudulent enlistment, and as you are a sworn law enforcement officer, we agreed to surrender him to you. With the understanding that you will immediately inform the sheriff's department."

"You mean while you're still here."

"Yes, ma'am." The Marine officer regarded Valkonen, made him as a cop. "You're not with the sheriff's department, are you, sir?"

Valkonen shook his head. "LAPD. But I'll put in a call for you, Lieutenant."

He called Chief Barton, who called the sheriff, and to be collegial also called Marletta Moses. The Marines were duly impressed at the clout the recruit's mother and her friend had. The sheriff brought with him Lieutenant Gelb, whom Joan had once likened to a Nazi, the lead detective working the drowning case. Gelb wanted to question Sebi privately, down at the station. The sheriff, in the interest of continuing cooperation with his fellow brass, said Sebi would be questioned right there in front of everyone. Assuming he didn't want to ask for a lawyer.

A look from his mother told Sebi he'd better not do that.

The Marines removed his handcuffs before he spoke.

It was a hard thing for a 16-year-old to do, look at all the powerful adults in the room, and make his confession. To his credit, Sebi looked at the person he figured would to be his harshest critic: his mother.

"It all started ... it started just being a date, that's all. The last one Audra ..." Giving voice to the girl's name made Sebi's throat close. He had to clear it before he could continue. "The last one we thought we'd ever have, after you told her parents what we did down in Mexico."

Joan winced at hearing her role in the tragedy.

"We went out to eat ... and then I said it'd be nice if we took one last walk on the beach. I swear to God, Mom, that's all I had in mind. So we drove out to Leo Carrillo. It was a little cloudy and cool and there was hardly anyone there when we arrived and nobody else after we'd walked a while. We hadn't said a word in twenty minutes and I was thinking the whole time we should just run away, the two of us, maybe go to Texas or Florida and start our lives together."

The picture that Sebi created in his mind brought tears to his eyes.

Joan could not keep from responding in kind.

"Then Audra said to me we should take one last swim together. I wasn't so sure about that. It was getting dark and the water looked cold. I think she saw I didn't want to, so she started taking off her clothes. She ran into the water. What was I supposed to do? I started getting undressed. While I was still taking my clothes off, she looked back at me and said if I caught her she'd do anything I wanted."

Valkonen listened to the boy closely. So far he hadn't heard one false note.

"I knew she was thinking I'd be thinking she meant sex. But what I was thinking was I'd catch her and then she'd have to run away with me. She said she'd do anything. I was going to hold her to that." Sebi sobbed and it was a minute before he could go on. "I knew I shouldn't have any trouble catching her. I'm a much better swimmer, but I was shocked how cold the water was. It slowed me down for a second. And then I heard Audra scream for help. It made me colder than I already was. I looked and I couldn't believe how far out she was. I knew right then she must've got caught in a rip.

"I swam out to her as fast as I could, but I kept losing sight of her; she kept going under. It seemed like I'd been swimming all night, but I finally got to her and kept her from going under that last time. It seemed like it took twice as long to get clear of the rip and bring her back to shore. I was so cold by then I was shaking. Audra was blue and she wasn't breathing."

Sebi's tears stopped and he seemed unaware of the others in the room with him. In a lifeless monotone, he continued. "As soon as I got Audra clear of the water, I did CPR on her. I tried and tried. But she never warmed up and she never started breathing. So I just, you know, put her legs together, covered her with her hands and hair. I looked for where we'd left our clothes. Found mine, but hers were gone. Somebody must've stolen them."

That was all Sebi had to say. Joan took him to his bedroom, not asking anyone's permission. She came back twenty minutes later. Ignoring Gelb, she spoke directly to the sheriff.

"Do you have any witnesses to contradict my son's account?"

"No, Detective."

"Any physical evidence that contradicts it?"

"No."

"Any evidence that supports it? Cracked ribs or sternum that someone receiving CPR from a frantic boy might suffer."

"Both ribs and sternum."

"And do you find my son's account credible?"

The sheriff nodded. "I think we all do, Detective. Please

bring your son in for a formal statement tomorrow and we'll close this case."

The sheriff said good night and left with a stone-faced Gelb.

The two chiefs left next and the Marines were about to go when Joan asked the officer to stay a moment. He told his men to wait for him downstairs and asked Joan how he might be of service. Valkonen watched silently from a corner.

"Is Sebi in any trouble with the Marine Corps, Lieutenant?"

"No, ma'am. We just try to make clear to the recruit, *impress him,* he better not enlist again before he's the right age. That's what I was getting at earlier. I'll file my report tomorrow. Sebastian should be just fine. He did a brave thing going after that poor girl."

"And the expense of the training he obtained fraudulently?"

"A cost of doing business, ma'am. With the good ones, we figure they'll come back to us when the time is right. I'm pretty sure your son will. Assuming you don't disagree."

"I want Sebi to go to college. He and I never talked about it before but maybe the Naval Academy would be good for him. He becomes a Marine, I want him to look like you."

Lieutenant Gervasio Chavez came to attention and snapped off a perfect salute.

"Thank you, Lieutenant."

"My pleasure, ma'am."

The Marine officer departed and that left only Duarte and Valkonen.

Joan said, "I'd go to church right now and light a hundred candles, except no way am I going to leave Sebi alone."

"I could do it for you. You sure you want a hundred?"

"I want a thousand. Half for Sebi, half for Audra. But a hundred's all I can afford."

"I'll make you a loan."

Joan smiled and looked as if she might cry again. "You're a great guy, Valkonen."

"Don't get all mushy on me, Detective."

"Once in a while, I might. You'll have to get used to it."

"Yeah?"

"What, you think this is the only time we'll work together?"

"Now that you mention it, probably not."

Joan kissed his cheek. Told him she had to call her family with the good news.

Valkonen slept in the Z parked down the block, in case his partner needed him.

About the Author

JOSEPH FLYNN is a Chicagoan, born and raised, currently living in central Illinois with his wife and daughter. Mr. Flynn is the author of *The Concrete Inquisition, Digger, The Next President,* and *Hot Type.*